The Danes

Sketched By Themselves

Vol.- I

by

Mrs. Bushby

Double 9 BOOKS

The Danes
Sketched By Themselves
Vol.- I
by Mrs. Bushby

ISBN: 978-93-60462-92-5

Published by

DOUBLE 9 BOOKS
2/13-B, Ansari Road
Daryaganj, New Delhi – 110002
info@double9books.com
www.double9books.com
Tel. 011-40042856

ABOUT THE AUTHOR

Mrs. Bushby, a great author, is acclaimed for the literary masterpiece "The Danes." In this exemplary work, Mrs. Bushby demonstrates a profound commitment to forging a meaningful connection between literature and fiction. The brilliance of the writer shines via as they craft narratives that cross beyond mere storytelling, aiming to facilitate a deeper know-how and connection amongst readers. Mrs. Bushby's writing is a testament to creativity and passion, as each paintings serves as a portal to diverse geographical regions of human experience. Through cautiously woven narratives, the writer introduces readers to a myriad of feelings and landscapes, developing a tapestry of storytelling that resonates with authenticity. The elegance of Mrs. Bushby's prose complements the literary enjoy, making the awesome memories both sophisticated and available. The writer's determination to bridging gaps in knowledge and fostering connections via literature is clear in every web page. Mrs. Bushby's writings are not just a collection of testimonies; they are a journey that invites readers to discover diverse facets of life and human emotion with entertainment and ease. In "The Danes" and past, Mrs. Bushby's legacy stands as a testament to the transformative electricity of literature in connecting humans and illuminating the human experience.

CONTENTS

COUSIN CARL FROM THE DANISH OF CARL BERNHARD

PART I

When I was a young man about twenty years of age, I was a sad hair-brained fellow. I lived entirely in the passing hour, the time gone by was quite forgotten, and about the future I never took the trouble to think a moment. Inclined to every possible species of foolish prank, I was always ready to rush headlong into any kind of frolic--anything that promised fun, even if that were a row; and never did I let slip the opportunity of amusing myself. I was a living proof that proverbs are not always infallible; for if 'bought wit is best,' that is to say, wisdom bought by experience, I must have become wise long ago; if 'a burned child or a scalded cat dreads the fire,' I was singed and scalded often enough to have felt some dread; and 'to pay the piper' had frequently fallen upon me. But I was none the wiser or more prudent. This preface was necessary in order to introduce the following episode of my mirth-loving youthful days.

My father thought that the best way of breaking off my intimacy with a somewhat riotous clique of young men, in whose jovial society I passed a good deal of my time, was to send me to Hamburg, where I was placed in the counting-house of a merchant, who was expected to keep a strict watch over me, on account of his well-known reputation for the most rigid morality; as if one could not find pleasant society in Hamburg if one were inclined to be gay! Before fourteen days had elapsed, I had at least three times outwitted the worthy man's vigilance, and twice out of these three times had not got home till close upon the dawn of day, without having been engaged in any fray; a pretty fair evidence that I sought good company, where the risk of getting a drubbing existed between the hours of one and three. But fate spread her protecting hand over me, and at the expiration of a year I returned safe and sound to Copenhagen, bringing back with me much experience in all manner of jolly diversions, and no small desire to carry my knowledge of them into continued practice.

I was of course destined to be bound hand and foot with the counting-house chains; but before putting them on I obtained leave to take a month's holiday in the country, and visit my uncles and my aunts in various parts of Zealand. One fine afternoon in the month of September, I sought out a common conveyance, such as is used by the peasantry, to take me the first few miles of my journey; and with my knapsack in my hand I was standing in the court-yard of the inn ready to step into the rustic carriage, when a servant entered the court and asked if there were any opportunity for Kjöge.

'That person standing there is going straight to Kjöge,' said the ostler of the inn.

The servant touched his hat. 'Here is a letter which it is of great consequence to my master should reach Kerporal's Inn at ----, where a private carriage will be waiting for him; he is not able to go where he is expected, as he has been taken ill. I would give the letter to the driver, but fear he might lose it.'

'Well, let me have it,' said I. 'I will be your master's messenger. What is his name?' He mentioned a name quite unknown to me. I pocketed the letter, and drove off.

My usual good luck did not attend me on this journey. In general I seldom drove a mile without meeting with some little adventure, if no better than taking up a passenger on the road, or mystifying some good-natured countryman, or playing the fool with some coquettish barmaid; but this time everything seemed bewitched, and I was tired to death. The Kjöge road is the stupidest of all possible roads--the wayfarers are too ragged and dirty for anyone to venture to take them up, the peasantry are deeper than coal-pits in cunning, and the barmaids are either as ugly as sin or engaged to the tapsters and cellarmen--in both cases disqualified for the situations they fill. I was dreadfully *ennuyé*, and, as if to add to my despair, one of the horses became lame, and they proceeded leisurely, step by step, at a snail's pace.

Whoever has felt as weary of his own company on a journey as I did, if he will put himself in my place, will not think it strange that I sometimes got out of the vehicle and walked, sometimes jumped in again, sometimes sang, sometimes whistled, sometimes thrust my hands into my pockets playing with everything there, then dragged them out and buttoned up my coat. But all this impatient rummaging in my pockets did no good to the stranger's letter, which became so crushed and crumpled that at last I discovered with some dismay that it looked more like a scrap of soiled paper than a respectable letter. It was in such a condition that it would be scarcely possible to deliver it--it was really almost in tatters. There was nothing to be done but to gain a knowledge of its contents, and deliver the same verbally to the coachman. Luckily the person who had sent it did not know who I was.

With the help of a little conjecture, I at length extracted from the maltreated epistle pretty much what follows:--

'Dear Uncle,--I have duly received your esteemed favour of the 7th instant, and see by it that my father had informed you of my arrival in Copenhagen by the steam-boat, and that you are so good as to say you would send your carriage to meet me on the 11th, about seven o'clock in the evening, at Kerporal's Inn, in order to convey me from thence to your house. A severe cold, which I caught on the voyage, obliges me to keep my room for the present, and to put off my visit to your dear unknown family for eight days or so. In making this communication I beg to assure you of my sincere regret at the delay, and to offer my best compliments to my beautiful cousins.' Then came one or two inflated and pedantic paragraphs, and the letter was subscribed

'Respectfully yours,

'Carl.'

The short and the long of the matter was that he would come in a week, being detained by a bad cold. 'Well, these interesting communications can be made in a few words to the coachman. It is surprising how much paper people think it necessary to waste when they want to trump up a reason for not doing anything!' With this sage remark I threw the letter down on the road, where it must speedily have become utterly illegible, for--one evil more--a shower came on, and it soon increased till the rain fell in torrents. Misfortunes, it is said, never come alone; on the contrary, pieces of good fortune seldom come in pairs.

At length we approached Kerporal's Inn. It was pouring of rain, it was eight o'clock, and it was already almost dark. A travelling-carriage was waiting under a shed, and its horses were stamping as if with impatience at a long detention. The gifts of fortune are surely very unequally distributed, methought, as I reflected on the solitary journey before me, and that it was impossible I could reach my uncle's parsonage until very late at night.

'To whom does that carriage belong?' I asked.

'It belongs to the Justitsraad,[1] at ---- Court,' replied the coachman. This place was situated about a mile[2] from my uncle's house.

'Oh! then it is you who are waiting for a gentleman from Copenhagen?' said I.

'Yes, sir. And since you are the gentleman, we had as well set off as fast as we can. The horses are baited, and we shall have no better weather this evening, sir,' said the coachman.

'Done!' thought I. 'This is not such a bad idea. I shall get so far dry and snugly; I can get out at the gate, or else carry the message myself. People are so hospitable in the country that they will surely offer me a night's lodging, and at an early hour to-morrow I shall proceed on foot to my uncle's house.' So the journey was not to be ended without an adventure.

It is pleasant to exchange a hard, wet conveyance, little better than a cart, which goes crawling along, for a comfortable carriage getting over the ground at a brisk pace; so I yielded to the temptation, and deposited myself in the latter, whilst I envied the pedant who could travel in such luxurious ease to beautiful unknown cousins--I who had neither equipages nor cousins--and he could stay at home to take care of his cold! *I* would not have done that in *his* place. The three miles[3] were soon got over--in fact, they did not seem more than one mile to me; for during the two last I was fast asleep, the carriage having rocked me into slumbers as gently as if it had been a cradle.

Suddenly it stopped, and as suddenly I awoke in a state of utter unconsciousness as to where I was. In a moment the door was opened, lights and voices around bewildered me still more, and I was almost dragged out of the carriage.

'It is he--it is cousin Carl!' was shouted in my ears, and the circle pressed more closely around me.

I was at ---- Court. I was about to execute my commission in the best manner I could, and make some apology for having brought the message myself instead of having delivered it to the coachman, when I spied a charming-looking little cousin, who thrust her pretty head forward with evident curiosity. How pretty she was! I could not take my eyes off of her, and stood staring at her for a moment in silence; but during that moment's silence I had been kindly welcomed by the family as 'Cousin Carl'--I who was only his unworthy messenger. Was I not in luck?

The Justitsraad carried me straight to the dining-room, and they sat down immediately to table, as if their repast had been retarded on my important account. I know not how I carried off my embarrassment; every moment my situation was becoming more and more painful; my spirits sank, and my usual effrontery ... ah! it failed me at the very time that I needed it most.

We were quite a family party. There were but the uncle; his wife, who was a pleasant, good-looking, elderly lady, apparently about fifty; cousin Jettè, who was pale and silent, but seemed very interesting; cousin Hannè, the charming little Venus who had caused my awkward position; and cousin Thomas, a lanky, overgrown boy, about twelve years of age, with long arms in jacket-sleeves too short for them. From sheer flurry I ate as if I had not seen food for a fortnight, and with each glass I emptied down my throat I started in my own mind one plan after another to escape from the dilemma into which my thoughtlessness had plunged me.

'I am very glad to see that you do not make strangers of us, but really are eating heartily,' said the Justitsraad as he filled my plate for the fifth time. 'I can't bear to see young men, or anyone, under restraint in my house; here everyone must do exactly as if he were at home. I am very glad you are not sitting like a stick, or looking as if you were afraid of us and of the viands before you. And now let us drink to your happy return to your native land. I am pleased to see that you are able now to pledge one in a glass of wine. When you were a boy, you had every appearance of turning out a regular milksop. But, to be sure, eleven years make great changes in everybody.'

I drank to the health of my father and mother, then to the welfare of the whole family, and then a special toast to cousin Jettè's health, which was proposed by her father himself. When we were about to drink it, he nodded to me with an air of intelligence, as if we were *d'accord* with each other; but the pretty cousin scarcely touched the glass with her lips, and did not vouchsafe me a single glance; it seemed as if she were far from pleased at the compliment paid her. Cousin Hannè, who sat near me, filled my glass every time it was empty, and she had so industriously employed herself in this manner, that my head was beginning to be a good deal confused.

'And now it is time to go to bed, my children!' said the Justitsraad. 'It is late; to-morrow we will hear all that your cousin has to tell us.'

I was on the point of requesting a moment's private conversation with him; but the moment for doing so passed away unseized--in the next it was no longer possible. The family bade each other good night, a servant showed me to my room, and I was left to my reflections. The reflections of a harum-scarum fellow of one-and-twenty! You are right, dear reader, they certainly were not worth much. Hannè's pretty face and the Justitsraad's good wine had taken a somewhat potent effect upon my brain; I hastened to seek repose, and, like the Theban tyrant, deferred grave business till the morrow.

But I could not fall asleep, for conscience plagued me; it is its custom to wake up when everybody is sleeping, and without the least mercy it compelled me to listen to its lectures. It became so importunate that it drove me out of bed, and induced me to admit that it would be better to jump out of the window, and carry my baggage on my shoulders to my uncle's parsonage, than to be treated to-morrow as an impudent puppy--*that* I should not so much mind--but also as a scamp of an impostor who had palmed himself upon them for the sake of obtaining a drive and a good supper gratis--*that* I should mind a great deal, for it would touch my honour. It is thus one reasons at twenty-one.

It rained no longer, but it was as dark as pitch. Darkness would favour my intention; but how was I to find my way in a place utterly unknown to me? I determined to keep awake till the dawn of day, then take myself off, and leave the family to make inquiries about the cousin, until the real one thought fit to recover from his cold. But that little Hannè's charming face, was I never to behold it again? Well, it was very foolish to have come there, but after all, it would be still more foolish to remain.

I left a little piece of my window open, and sat down near it in order to watch for the first streaks of daylight. I had, however, a long time to wait, for it was just half-past twelve o'clock. As I sat there, fretting at myself for my folly, I heard something or some one, stirring beneath the window, and a moment afterwards among the branches of a tree close by. It was some person climbing the tree, but his visit was not intended for me, for he crept up much higher, and appeared to have mounted to a level with an upper window, as one was opened very gently and cautiously. Ah! an assignation! a secret appointment!

It is really an advantage to have a tender conscience; without that I should have been fast asleep, and should never have known what was going on so near me. But who could it be? Could cousin Thomas, though only twelve years of age, be making love to one of the housemaids? Let us listen.

'For God's sake make no noise!' said a whispering voice at the window above mine. 'He has arrived; he occupies the room just below, and he can hardly be asleep yet.'

'The light has been extinguished for at least half an hour,' replied the voice in the tree. 'Such an ape has nothing to wake or watch for.'

An ape, forsooth! as if I were not quite as wide awake as himself.

'Dear Gustav, think of my distress,' continued the voice at the window; 'my father drank my health at table, and nodded to him in such a significant manner! Oh, how I hate that man! Tomorrow, perhaps, he will begin to treat me as his betrothed; my father will give him every opportunity, and he will take upon himself to be intimate, and to make me presents. Oh! how unhappy I am!'

'You see, dearest Jettè, this is the consequence of our silence; if we had spoken to him before the accursed cousin came here, perhaps your father might have been persuaded to have given up this absurd childish betrothal.'

'No--no; he would never have done that,' replied Jettè; 'he is too much attached to his brother; and he will do everything in his power to have the agreement fulfilled, which eleven years ago they entered into with each other at their children's expense.'

'Why did not that man break his neck on the way! Such fellows can travel round the whole world without the slightest accident ever happening to them,' said Gustav. 'But he may, perhaps, repent coming here; I shall pick a quarrel with him, I will call him out, he shall fight with me, and either he or I shall be put out of the way.'

'May God protect you, my dearest Gustav!' exclaimed my cousin. 'But how can you have the heart to frighten me with such threats? Am I not wretched enough? Would you increase the burden that is weighing me down to the grave? I see nothing before me but misery and despair; no comfort--no escape.' Poor Jettè was weeping; I could hear how she sobbed in her woe. I now perceived why the poor girl had been so pale and distant--I was betrothed to her.

'Forgive me, dearest girl! I hardly know what I am saying; but take comfort, do not weep so bitterly. Heaven will not desert us, and we shall find some means of softening your father; besides, no rational man would wish to obtain a wife upon compulsion. If he has the least pride or spirit, he will himself draw back.'

'Ah, Gustav! if there were any chance of his drawing back, he would not have come here. His father wrote that he was coming expressly to claim his--his promised rights; and that--and that we should learn to know each other before the wedding. We had been betrothed for eleven years, he wrote, and it was time that ... No! I cannot think of it without despair.'

'What sort of looking person is he? Is he handsome? Whom does he resemble?'

'He is not in the least like what he was as a boy, he is very much changed; he has improved very much in looks, and, indeed, may be called handsome now.'

'That is a girl with a good taste,' thought I; 'I wish I could help her out of her troubles.'

'Handsome!--I congratulate you, Miss Jettè--handsome people generally make a favourable impression, and by degrees one becomes quite reconciled to them, and pleased with them--don't you think so?'

The lover grasped the branch nearest him so roughly in his anger, that he made the whole tree shake.

'Gustav! are you in earnest?' exclaimed Jettè, in a tone of voice that would have gone to the heart of a stone, if stones had hearts.

'Dearest, dearest Jettè! Sweet, patient angel!' He stretched himself so far out from the tree that I think he must have reached her hand and kissed it.

'Indeed, you have no reason to be jealous of him,' said Jettè, 'for one quite forgets his being handsome, when one observes how awkward he is. He does not seem to be at all accustomed to society; he eats like a shark, and you should have seen how he drank. Hannè amused herself in filling his glass, and I do believe that for his own share alone he emptied two bottles of wine. And he never uttered a single word. Oh! he is my horror--that man; but my father seems pleased with him, and praised him after he had left the room. Dear Gustav! how unfortunate we are!'

Should I allow these imputations to rest upon me? A blockhead--a glutton--and a drunkard! And cousin Hannè had been making a fool of me, forsooth!--the little jade, with her pretty face. I was certainly in a pleasant position.

'I will speak to your father to-morrow,' said Gustav, after a little consideration. 'He is very fond of you, he will not be deaf to our prayers, or expect impossibilities from you. What can he bring forward against me? I shall soon be in a position to maintain a wife, my family are quite on an equality with his own, my father is not poor, and my situation in life is now, and always will be, such, that I can satisfy any inquiry he can make into it. Deny then no longer your consent, dearest Jettè; let us no longer conceal our attachment from him, and depend on it all will go well.'

'Ah, Gustav! you do not know my father. He will positively insist that I shall fulfil this engagement. Vows are sacred in his eyes, and he himself has never broken his word. When I gave that promise I was but a child, and I wore the plain gold ring without ever reflecting that it was a link of that never-to-be-broken chain which was to bind me to a life of misery. Oh, God, have mercy upon me!'

'Doubt not *His* help, my beloved girl! He will spread His protecting hand over us, even if all else shall fail us.'

The sorrowing lovers whispered then so softly that I could not overhear what further they said, but I concluded they were comforting each other.

The first streak of day cast a pale line of light across the tops of the trees and the roofs of the outhouses near. It was almost time for me to commence *my* flight, but everything must be quiet first. I gathered together my effects with as little noise as possible. The conversation on the outside recommenced, and I approached the window impatiently.

'How long is he going to stay here?' asked Gustav.

'I do not know; perhaps only a few days. Alas! my only hope is in him,' replied Jettè. To-morrow I shall have a private conversation with him, which, of course, will lead to an explanation. I will make an appointment with him in the garden,--if you will promise me not to be jealous,' added Jettè, with a degree of archness in her tone which enchanted me.

'It is hard that my rival is to be my sheet anchor,' said Gustav; 'but, since it must be so, speak to him, dearest. However, if that fails, then, my sweet girl, then ...'

'Then I promise you ... But what noise is that? I thought I heard some one stirring. For God's sake go! Let no one see you here!'

'To-morrow night, then, at one o'clock. Farewell, dear Jettè.'

Then came a kiss. Was it on the hand or the lips?

'Take care how you get down. To-morrow night. Adieu till then!'

The faithful knight-errant swung himself from branch to branch with an adroitness which proved that he was experienced in that mode of descent. As soon as he set foot on the ground the window above was closed.

It was now my turn to get into the trees. Gustav had taught me that trick. I wondered what sort of a looking fellow he was. Poor Jettè--to have chosen for herself, and yet to be condemned to be sacrificed to a man who could begin a letter about his intended bride with, 'I have duly received your esteemed favour of the 5th instant,' and who could absent himself from such a charming girl, merely because he had a slight cold! Well! it is a wretched world, this, in which we live. It was becoming more and more light. To-day she wished to have a private conversation with me--her only hope was in me; there was to be an explanation between us, an assignation in the garden. Who the deuce could run away from all this? But.... Well! nobody knew me--the real cousin was not coming for a week ... surely I might stay *one* day on the strength of personifying him? I am a fatalist; destiny has sent me, and it will aid me.... I will not forsake Jettè ... and I will revenge myself upon that little Mademoiselle Hannè, who wanted to drink me under the table, and I will show the whole accomplished family that I have studied good manners in Hamburg, and am neither a blockhead, a glutton, nor a drunkard. It is a matter that touches my honour; I will stay!... But ... suppose they take it into their heads to question me? Humph! If the worst comes to the worst, I can but stuff a little linen into my great-coat pocket, make a pretext to get outside the gate, and take to flight at once. In the meantime, I will make some inquiries about the neighbourhood and the roads, for at present I have not the most remote idea whether I ought to turn to the right hand or the left. And to-morrow night--good-by to this darling family, with many thanks for their kind welcome. Whilst they are all sleeping, or keeping nocturnal assignations, I shall vanish without leaving the slightest trace behind. It will give them something to talk of till Christmas.

Whilst this monologue was in progress of utterance, I was busily undressing myself. I jumped into bed, and soon slept as soundly as if I had a lawful right to be there, and were the dreaded cousin himself.

But when I was summoned to breakfast next morning I was in a very different frame of mind. I had slept off the effects of the wine, sober reason had resumed her sway, fear followed at my heels like a bad spirit; and I would assuredly have made my escape if the well-dressed valet-de-chambre had left me a moment to myself. I was compelled to resign myself to my fate, and allow myself to be marshalled to the breakfast-parlour; but as I approached the scene of my threatened exposure, despair restored my courage, I remembered that it was incumbent on me to wipe out the disgrace of the preceding evening, and I found my habitual impudence and lightness of heart upon the very threshold of the door.

I went up to them all, and shook hands with them, and as I now knew that I was engaged to Jettè, I kissed her hand with all possible amorous gallantry. The poor girl looked as if she could have sunk into the earth, and I coloured up to my temples, for I just recollected that I had on no betrothal ring. Jettè wore the plain gold ring I had heard her mention, but it was almost hidden by another ring, with a simple enamelled 'Forget-me-not.' Might not *that* have been a gift from the unknown Gustav?

'How are you this morning, my dear?' said the Justitsraad. 'Jettè has not been very well lately,' he added; 'she looks poorly, and has no appetite. It must be that abominable *nervousness*, of which young ladies now-a-days are always complaining.'

Jettè assured him that she felt quite well. I doubted if her mother or her sister were so much in her confidence as I was at that moment; but neither of them had been sitting at an open window between twelve o'clock at night and three o'clock in the morning.

At first all went on smoothly, for the conversation was on the safe subjects of wind and weather; but a change for the worst was coming.

'Now, nephew, tell us something about the old people yonder. How is my brother looking?'

'Extremely well, uncle. He is looking quite fresh.'

'But the gout--the gout in his feet? that sticks to him yet--and it is not the most pleasant of companions.'

'Oh, yes--the gout! But he is accustomed to that.'

'And your mother?'

'She is also well, only she is getting older every day.'

'Ah! that is what we are all doing. And aunt Abelonè? How goes it with her?'

'She is very well too.'

'What! *very well*--with her broken leg! Why, you must be joking?'

'Oh dear, no! I ... I only meant to say as well ... as well as anyone can be with a broken leg,' I stammered out. In truth, I knew nothing about, and cared as little for, Abelonè's mishap.

'Listen to that madcap. He speaks of a broken leg as if it were absolutely a trifling matter.'

The danger was over for a moment, but another attack soon followed. I had scarcely swallowed a cup of tea, before my *soi-disant* uncle demanded from me a particular account of the new system of agriculture my father had introduced on his property--I, who did not even know where that property lay! But this time his wife came to the rescue, for she declared that we could discuss systems of husbandry when we were strolling in the fields together, or out hunting, and that she and her daughters did not take much interest in agricultural questions.

'Well, we will talk of this another time,' said the Justitsraad. 'But tell us at present something of your travels. Women-folk are always pleased to hear adventures of travellers. You have visited Paris, Berlin, Vienna, and many other places. A man who has travelled so much might talk for a whole month without being at a loss for a subject.'

Very well did I know that I had never beheld a single building either in Paris or Berlin, except in engravings. What was I to say? I busied myself in getting up a good tale.

'Upon my word, nephew, I should not suspect you of being very bashful; but if you don't like to speak of your travels, let them alone, my boy,--everybody shall do as he likes in my house. Many years ago, I remember, I went to Hamburg, and when I came home I almost tired them all out by describing what I had seen. But I suppose it is old-fashioned now to make any comments on what one has witnessed abroad.'

Here was a piece of good luck. I knew Hamburg as well as my own pockets, and now I was like my uncle after *his* return. There was no end to my descriptions and anecdotes. The old man seemed to take real delight in hearing about all the alterations which had been made in the old town since the days of his youth, inquiring often for places which no longer exist. I endeavoured to make my discourse as amusing as possible. Cousin Thomas rested his elbows on the table, listened with open mouth, and laughed outright several times; my aunt often let her knitting-needle fall, to look at the pencil sketches with which I was illustrating my descriptions; cousin Jettè looked less sourly at me than before; and Hannè--the pretty, coquettish, little Hannè--for whose sake I was sitting apparently so much at my ease among them, was unwearied in her queries about the Hamburg ladies, fashions, and theatres. Happily these had been the objects of my most intense study.

'I perceive now, that when once his tongue is set a-going, he has plenty to say,' remarked my worthy uncle. 'How long were you in Berlin?'

'Nay; stop, uncle! we are at Hamburg just now. I have still a great deal to tell about that city. Everything should be arranged in due order. Today I will confine myself to Hamburg; to-morrow we shall travel to Berlin.' 'Catch me here tomorrow,' thought I to myself; 'if I only can get through to-day, I will take French leave before we come to Berlin.'

'Come! since you give such a good reason, we will let you off Berlin just now. I am a lover of order myself, and here everything goes by clockwork. During the first part of the morning every one must look out for himself; at twelve we meet for luncheon--at three o'clock we dine. Amuse yourself in the mean time as well as you can; you will find plenty of books in the library--yonder hang fire-arms--and in the stables there are horses at your service; do exactly as if you were at home, and take care of yourself.'

'I will take a turn in the garden,' said I, with a glance at Jettè--one of those looks *d'intelligence* from which I expected great things; but she took no notice of it, and I was under the necessity of remarking, that being a stranger I did not know the way. But even this opening for a *tête-à-tête* she allowed to pass, and I could not imagine how she intended to bring about our secret conference.

'A stranger!' cried my uncle. 'But true, in eleven years one forgets a great deal. Let me see--how old were you then? you are three-and-twenty now ... twelve years of age you were; who could have guessed then that you would have become such a free-and-easy, off-hand sort of a fellow? Well, let him be shown the grounds, children. Thomas must go to his studies; my wife has her household matters to attend to; Jettè, you must ...'

'I really am not able, my dear father--I have a dreadful headache,' said the poor timid girl. And she looked as if she spoke nothing but the truth,--she was so pale, and her eyes were so red.

'A woman's malady,' said her father, looking vexed; 'it is, of course, incumbent on you to ... Well; all that will vanish when you are better acquainted. *We* know what these qualms mean,' he added, turning towards me. I nodded, as if I would have said--*Sat sapienti*. 'Have you also got a headache, Hannè? Are you also suffering from nervousness? or can you stand the fresh morning air, my girl?' he asked. I looked eagerly at the little gipsy.

'Oh! I can endure the fresh morning air very well,' she replied.

'Then take charge of your cousin Carl, and show him round the garden and the shrubberies; and don't forget the pretty view from the rising ground where the swing is.'

The Justitsraad held out his hand to me, and I pressed it with all the warmth of sincere gratitude.

'Come, cousin,' said Hannè. 'Shall we call each other by our first names, or not? But we can settle that as we go along.'

'For Heaven's sake, let us call each other by our baptismal names, else we should not seem like cousins. Don't you think so, uncle?'

'You are of my own people, my boy. Always be merry and frank--that is my motto. I am right glad that you have not adopted the stiff German manners. Your father was always very grave; but you have rubbed off all that solemnity abroad, I am happy to see.'

In my delight at the promised stroll with Hannè, I forgot that it was my duty to kiss Jettè's hand on leaving her. Just as I had reached the door I suddenly remembered it; and rushing back, I went through the salutation in the speediest manner possible, expressing at the same time my hope to find her better on my return. They all laughed, and even Jettè could not help smiling,--there was something so comical in my hurried return, and equally hurried performance of the ceremony etiquette demanded.

Was I not right in calling myself a madcap? Here was I actually walking with the charming little Hannè all over the grounds! I--her pretended cousin;

I--who ought to have been sent to the House of Correction, for having, under another man's name, presumed to thrust myself into the midst of a respectable family; I--who had committed, a positive depredation, and broken the sacred privacy of a seal;--here was I wandering about arm-in-arm with the Justitraad's daughter at ---- Court, the captivating, innocent, beautiful little Hannè; I--who deserved to be driven away with all the dogs on the estate at my heels! Well! goodness and justice do not always carry the day in this world!

PART II

When I looked at my companion I was almost appalled at my audacity. Think of the face you love the best in this world--the face that you never can behold without a beating heart--which you dwell on with rapture, which is the object of your waking and your sleeping dreams! Ah! quite as charming as such looked Hannè in her pink gingham morning-dress, with a little blue handkerchief tied carelessly round her throat, and a becoming white bonnet. She was irresistible!

We strayed here and there like two children; plucked flowers to teach each other their botanical names; gathered a whole handful to commence a herbarium, and threw them away again to chase some gaudy butterfly. Then we sauntered on slowly, and Hannè communicated many little things to me of which she thought her cousin ought to be informed; and at length I began to fancy that I actually was the real cousin Carl. Of all the young girls that ever I beheld, Hannè was the most delightful; such grace, such vivacity, such naïveté, were not to be met with either in Copenhagen or in Hamburg.

'It is a pity Jettè could not accompany you,' said she; 'but to-morrow, probably, her headache will be gone.'

I assured her that I did not regret Jettè's absence, since I had *her* company.

'That is a pretty declaration from a bridegroom who has allowed himself to be waited for eleven years,' said Hannè.

'Jettè did not look as if she were glad at my arrival.'

'You must not think anything of that; she has looked out of spirits for a month past, at least: she is apt to be melancholy at times, but it passes off. Her character is sedate. She is much better, therefore, than I am, or than anyone I know. You can hardly fancy how good she is.'

'But I want a lively wife, for I am myself of a very gay disposition,' said I.

'That is not what we thought you were,' replied my fair companion. 'We always looked upon you as a quiet, grave, somewhat heavy young man, and you have been described to us as a most tedious, wearisome person. I used often to pity Jettè in my own mind; for a stupid, humdrum man is the greatest bore on earth. But I do not pity her anymore, now.'

I could have kissed her, I was so pleased.

'So you thought of me with fear and disgust, you two poor girls? Pray, who painted my portrait so nicely?'

'Why, your own father did; and the letter which you wrote Jettè when she was confirmed, and when you sent her the betrothal-ring, did not at all improve our opinion of you. I'll tell you what, Carl; that was a miserable epistle. It was with the utmost difficulty that my father prevailed on Jettè to answer it, when she was obliged to send you a ring in return. However, you were little more than a boy then--it is long ago, and it was all forgotten when we never heard again from you. I can venture to affirm that Jettè has not thought six times about you in the six years that have elapsed since that time--and perhaps this is lucky for you. It was not until your father wrote us that you had come home, and until he began to bombard Jettè with presents and messages from you, that you were mentioned again among us; but my father never could bear our laughing at your renowned epistle.'

I listened with the utmost avidity to every little circumstance that could elucidate the part I had taken upon myself to play. In this conversation I learned more than I could have gathered the whole morning.

'It is very absurd to betroth children to each other. What should they know of love?' said Hannè.

'It is more than absurd, Hannè; it is positive barbarity. It is trampling the most sacred feelings and rights under foot.'

'Nevertheless you may thank God for that barbarity,' said she; 'without it you would never have got Jettè. She has plenty of admirers.'

'Indeed! And who are they, if I may take the liberty of asking? You make me quite jealous.'

'Oh, I have observed that both the young clergyman at ---- Town and Gustav Holm are much attached to her. And Jettè has no dislike to Gustav.'

'Who is Gustav Holm? He appears to be the most dangerous.'

'He is learning farming, or rather, I ought to say, agricultural affairs, with a country gentleman not far from this. He has been coming to our house now about three years; I think, and I could wager a large sum, that it is for Jettè's sake.'

'Or for your own, little Hannè?'

'Pshaw! nonsense! If anyone were dangling here after me, I should make no secret of it. Jettè is a greater favourite than I am, and she deserves to be so.'

'But perhaps Jettè cares more for Gustav Holm than for me, whom she really does not know?'

One often asks a question in this hypocritical world about what one knows best oneself.

'No, oh no! That would be a sad affair. Has she not been engaged to you for eleven years, and is she not going to be married to you?'

'But if you had been in Jettè's place, how would you have felt?'

'I would perhaps have preferred ... No, I don't think I would though. But I am not so mild and amiable as Jettè; and the day that I was confirmed no one should have imposed a betrothal-ring upon me, I can assure you, sir; and, least of all, accompanied by such an elegant billet as yours.'

Hannè picked up a blade of grass, formed it into a string, and twisting it round her finger in an artistic manner, made it into a knot.

'Can you make such?' said she.

I tried it, but could not succeed, and she took hold of my hand to do it for me.

'But how is this, Carl?' she exclaimed. 'Where is your betrothal-ring?'

'It is ... I have ... I wear it attached to a ribbon round my neck; ... it annoyed me to have to answer the many questions it was the cause of my being asked. Therefore I determined to wear it near my heart.'

'It annoyed you! Did ever anyone hear such an assertion? Jettè has faithfully worn hers, and placed a "*Forget-me-not*"; into the bargain by its side, to remind herself, I suppose, not to forget you. But *you* found it a bore, even to be asked if you were engaged! Such gallants as you do not deserve to be remembered. But come now, I will show you a beautiful view.'

We passed together through a charming shady wood, where several paths, diverging among the trees, crossed each other. Hannè walked before, light and graceful as Diana in her fluttering drapery; I followed her, like the enamoured Actæon. Alas! the resemblance would soon become stronger, I thought--how soon might I not be discovered, driven forth as a miserable intruder, and delivered over to regret and remorse, which would prey upon me, and tear me to atoms, as the hounds tore Actæon!

Upon a rising ground stood a swing, the posts of which towered above the tops of the trees, and the erection looked at a distance like a gallows.

From this spot the view was very extensive--a number of country churches could be seen from it, and among others that of my uncle.

'But why have you placed that gallows upon this lovely spot?' I asked.

'Gallows! No one ever presumed to give such an appellation to my swing before,' said Hannè, angrily. 'If it were not very uncivil, I would say that it evinces an extremely debased and disordered state of the imagination to make a gallows out of my innocent swing.'

The girl spoke the absolute truth. It will hereafter come to be called gallows, thought I--and tomorrow my fair fame will hang dangling there, as a terror and a warning to all counterfeit cousins.

'But never mind, cousin, I did not mean to be so sharp with you. Don't, however, let my father hear you say anything disparaging of this place; he would not so easily forgive you. Come, you shall atone for your sin by swinging me,' added Hannè, as she settled herself in the swing.

'Ah, Hannè! would that I could as easily atone for all my sins towards you!'

I could have swung her for a lifetime, I do believe, without becoming weary of gazing at her; but she compassionately stopped, fancying I must be tired.

'You will be quite fatigued, poor fellow--it would be a shame to make you work longer,' said she. 'Get in, and you shall find that the swing stands in a good situation; that is to say, if you are not afraid of the gallows,' she added, as she made room for me.

'For your sake, I would not shun even the gallows,' said I, as I sprang up.

The swing went at full speed; it was pleasant to be carried thus over the tops of the trees, and behold the earth as if stretched out beneath one's feet. I felt as if in heaven. I was flying in the air with an angel.

'How delightful this is!' I cried, throwing my arm round Hannè's waist.

'What, to be on a gallows? But pray hold on by the rope, cousin, and not by me. Now let us get down--we have had enough of this pastime.'

'I have an earnest prayer to make to you, dear Hannè,' I said, seizing her hand. 'Listen to me before we leave this place. I foresee that the swing, at least in your recollection, will retain the name I accidentally gave it. Promise me that you will come here when you hear evil of me, and doubt my honour, and that you will then remember that it was here I entreated you to judge leniently of the absent. Fate plays strange tricks with us, dear

Hannè; it throws us sometimes into temptations which we are too weak to withstand. Promise me that you will not condemn me irrevocably, although appearances may be against me.'

The lovely girl looked at me for a moment with surprise and earnestness, and then suddenly burst into an immoderate fit of laughter; another moment, and my confession would have been made.

'I promise you,' said she, 'that I shall come here and think of you as well as you deserve--that is to say, if I have nothing else to do, and nothing else to think of. But at present I have no time to spare for gallows'-reflections, the bell is ringing for luncheon, and my father likes us to appear punctually at table.'

Jettè did not come down to luncheon, her headache confined her to her room, poor girl! I felt very sorry for her, and when I reflected that my principal, whose unworthy messenger I was, would torment her still more, my heart really grieved for her. The family were very cheerful, and it was long since I had been among so pleasant and sociable a little party. Alas! half the day was now gone, and when the other half were passed it would be all over with my enjoyments.

After luncheon, cousin Thomas came to me and begged that I would go out with him for a few hours' shooting, the afternoon being his time for exercise and amusement. I wished to be on good terms with all the family, and therefore accepted his invitation; besides, I thought he might be in a talkative humour, and that I might be able to extract from him some particulars of their domestic history. We took a couple of guns and sallied forth. I had already become so hardened that I did not feel the slightest twinge of conscience at thus abusing the open-hearted confidence of twelve years of age. 'Give the Devil an inch, and he will take an ell,' says the proverb.

But cousin Thomas was too keen a sportsman to have ears for anything except sporting anecdotes, and I soon began to grudge the time I had wasted upon him. There was no help for me, however. I was in for it, and I had to follow him from one moor to another, removing myself every moment farther from his father's abode.

'Who is that person yonder?' I asked by mere chance, only not to seem quite silent.

'Where? Oh! that is Gustav Holm,' said Thomas. 'He is coming, I dare say, from Green Moor--the very best moor in the whole neighbourhood.'

'We must speak to him.--Mr. Holm! Mr. Holm! Good morning, Mr. Holm.'

The person thus hailed stopped for a moment, and then came up to us. I forthwith introduced myself as a newly-arrived relative of the family at ---- Court, and he cast on me the pleasant glance with which one generally eyes a rival.

'What sort of sport have they to-day at Green Moor?' I asked; and I attacked him with questions and stuck to him like a burr, though I saw that he would fain have got rid of me. But that was impossible. Mr. Holm was exceedingly chary of his words; therefore if either was a blockhead, as I had been described the night before, it was he rather than I.

'I will do poor Jettè a service while I can,' thought I; and I invited Mr. Holm to return with us to ---- Court. 'You visit at my uncle's, I think,' I added; 'it strikes me that I have heard my cousin speak of you.'

He grew as red as fire, poor fellow.

'I don't think little Hannè will pick a quarrel with me because I beg you to accompany us home,' said I, slily; and the luckless lover became still more embarrassed. He tried to excuse himself, but I would take no denial; he was obliged to give way, and in triumph I brought my prisoner back with me. 'Thomas will bear witness to the ladies how much trouble I had in prevailing on you to come, and they will therefore the more highly appreciate your self-sacrifice,' said I.

When we reached the gate, he tried again to negotiate for his freedom, but Thomas found his reluctance so amusing, that he would not allow him to make his escape. Giving way at length, he exclaimed,

'You are going to afflict your party with a tiresome addition, for I have a dreadful headache to-day.'

'You will feel better when you have dined,' I replied; 'and if you would like to have some sal volatile, you can get some from my *fiancée*; she has a headache also to-day. There must be something in the air to cause it, since you are similarly affected.'

Mr. Holm evidently writhed under my mode of treatment; and at the term *fiancée* he looked as if I had trodden heavily upon his corns. It was certainly very trying, but I had comfort in the background for him.

Neither the Justitsraad nor his wife seemed to be much pleased at the arrival of their unexpected guest; nevertheless, they received him politely, and assigned to him a place at table between them. He could not have demanded a more honourable seat. Thomas was inexhaustible in his descriptions of Mr. Holm's unwillingness to give himself up as a captive, and how clever he had been in securing him. Poor Jettè dared hardly look up from her plate.

'Mr. Holm ought to know that he is always welcome,' said the Justitsraad; but it was evident that the remark was the result of good breeding, rather than of any cordial pleasure he had in seeing him.

'Very true, uncle; that is just what I said. Hannè spoke of him to me so highly this morning, that I really became quite eager to make his acquaintance. The friends of the family must also be my friends. I knew right well that Hannè would not be angry at me if I brought him home with me.'

'I! What did I say?' exclaimed Hannè, colouring deeply. 'How can you make such an assertion? I believe ...'

'That I am a sad gossip, and never can keep to myself what I hear--I confess the truth of the impeachment.'

Her parents looked at her with surprise; Jettè cast an inquiring glance towards her, and Gustav forced a smile. Hannè was very angry, but her wrath did not last long; time was precious to me, and I speedily effected a reconciliation with her.

'I do verily believe that you are not quite sober to-day, Carl,' said Hannè in a whisper to me, when we rose from table.

'Truth to tell, Hannè, I am not, but that is your fault. Why did you try to make me drink myself under the table last night? It is only a judgment from Heaven on you; those who dig a pit for other people often fall into it themselves.'

'Hark ye, cousin! I am very near wishing that you had been in reality as stupid a nonentity as we were given to understand you were.'

'What if you should be taken at your word? You may get your wish more easily than you imagine; by this day week the transformation may have been brought about; see if you don't wish me back again then.'

Her father took my arm, and proposed adjourning to the garden with our cigars. I had nearly fled the field at this invitation, so much did I dread a *tête-à-tête* with him; nothing on earth could have detained me but the expected secret meeting with Jettè, whose good genius I was to be. I felt that I could almost rather have faced his Satanic Majesty himself at that moment, had the choice between the two companions been mine; but what was I to do? There was nothing for it but to accompany my host quietly.

'Listen, my son,' said the old gentleman, when we had exhausted our first cigars; 'I cannot say I am much pleased at your having brought that

Mr. Holm back with you. He is a very respectable young man, but ... Why should we encumber ourselves with him?... To speak out, you should have been the last person to have brought *him* to this house.'

'*I!* How so? I really had planned to make him one of my most intimate friends. Hannè said so much in his favour.'

'Hannè does not care a straw for him--she is only a child.'

'A child! and on the 12th of November she will be seventeen years old! No, no, uncle, girls give up thinking themselves children when they arrive at ten years of age.'

'But I tell you, Hannè does not care in the least for him; nor does he for her.'

'Very well, uncle, so much the better, for there is no sort of danger then in his coming here.'

'Danger! Oh! I don't look upon him as at all dangerous; but I can't bear to see him looking so woe-begone.'

'I shall soon enliven him. Only leave him to me, and you will see that he shall become quite gay. I will take him in hand if he can come here every day.'

'Confound the fellow! I must just tell you plainly out then--he is a great admirer of Jettè. Do you understand me now?'

'May I ask how you know that, sir?'

'How I know that?... Well ... No matter how. Suffice it to say, I know it. Jettè cannot endure him, that I know also; but his sighs might make some impression on her, so it were better that he kept entirely away. Besides, if he gets no encouragement, his fancy will wear out. Don't you agree with me that he had better not come here?'

'I can't call it a sin to be in love with Jettè, for I am so myself; she is a girl that it would be impossible not to admire. If we were to drive away every one who was guilty of admiring her, we should be compelled at last to live as hermits.'

'What the devil, nephew! Do *you* say all this--you, who are to be her future husband?'

'One must be somewhat liberal, uncle--one must seem not to observe everything. Suspicion does a great deal of harm, and jealousy would only encourage the evil. Jettè shall find me as gentle as a lamb. Besides, you have assured me that she cannot endure him.'

'Well!... Perhaps she does not exactly hate him ... she has no particular fault to find with him ... but he embarrasses her ... he embarrasses her ... and when a person embarrasses one ...' The good man had got into a dilemma, and he was not able to get out of it; so he stopped short.

'Oh! that will pass off when she accustoms herself to see him. It is a great misfortune to let oneself be embarrassed by the presence of others; really, after a time this would lead one to become a misanthrope--a hater of one's species.'

The Justitsraad looked at me with astonishment, while he replied:

'I wish you had not gone on your travels; I fear your morality has suffered not a little in consequence. I hardly knew you again, you are so much changed. You are not like the same being who, eleven years ago, was such a quiet, bashful boy. And your father, who constantly wrote that you were not the least altered, he must scarcely recognize you himself.'

'That is very probable, uncle, for I hardly know myself again. But travelling abroad is sure always to make some little change in people.'

'It must have been Berlin that has done the mischief, and made such a transformation in you; for the letters your father sent me, which you had written from Vienna, did not in the slightest degree lead me to imagine that you had become such a hair-brained, thoughtless fellow.'

'True enough it is that I am thoughtless and hair-brained, but, believe me, I have never been guilty of any deliberate wrong. I know I am too often carried away by the impulse of the moment, and too often forget what may be the consequences.'

'One must make some allowance for youth,' replied the old gentleman. 'So it was at Berlin you studied folly in all its branches--Berlin, which I had always believed to be a most correct and exemplary city, whither one might send a young man without the least risk! Well, well! let us consign to oblivion all the pranks you must have played to have been metamorphosed from a milksop to a madcap. We must all sow our wild oats some time or other, and I hope you have sown yours, and are done with them.'

'No, indeed, I fear not; on the contrary, I feel that I am in the midst of that period; but I promise you that it shall soon be over, and that then nothing shall tempt me to such follies. As to youthful imprudence, if it be not carried too far, I shall rely upon your indulgence. Will you not wink a little at it, and let your kind, generous heart plead for me when your reason might condemn me?'

'You are a queer fellow, nephew, and a wild one, I fear; but it is not possible to be angry with you.'

'Would to Heaven that you may always be inclined to entertain such friendly feelings towards me!' I replied, as I pressed his hand. There was good reason for my bespeaking his indulgence; it would be amply required the very next day.

I skilfully managed to bring the subject back to Gustav Holm, and soon perceived that he had really nothing to say against him. Holm's position was good in all respects, and the old gentleman would have considered him a very good match for one of his daughters, if he had not had another project in his head. But he had set his heart so entirely on the family alliance, that he could not admit the idea of any other. In eleven years there had been time for it to become deeply rooted in his mind.

When we sought the rest of the party, we found them all standing round the swing. Hannè was busy attaching a piece of paper to one of the poles.

'What are you doing there, child?' asked her father.

'It is Carl's name which I am putting on the gallows, as a well-deserved punishment for all the follies of which he has been guilty in word and deed to-day,' she replied, continuing her employment. 'Only think, he disgraced my swing by pretending to mistake it for a gallows. So there stands his name; and there it shall stand, to his eternal shame and reproach, and in ridicule of him when he is gone. We must have something to recall him to our recollection.'

'Nemesis,' thought I, 'already!' I was as much moved inwardly, as the worthy emperor, Charles V., must have been when he witnessed his own funeral. Humph! no one likes jesting about such serious matters. Who knows in what it might end?

We amused ourselves with swinging--we chattered nonsense, or discoursed gravely--we sauntered about, all together or in groups by turns. Hannè was the life of the party, and by degrees everyone seemed to partake of her gaiety. Even Jettè talked more. I had seized on the unhappy lover, and held him fast by the arm, in the charitable intention of bringing him near his lady-love, without anyone's remarking his proximity to her; but the overcautious girl avoided us, and Gustav himself had not courage to begin a conversation on different subjects. I was quite distressed about them, poor things! 'We must try what can be done in the wood,' thought I; 'there are paths enough in it, the party will become more scattered, and I shall then be able to manage, perhaps, to get them into some secluded spot.' But our progress was arrested by a servant, who came to announce that some visitors had arrived.

Visitors! At that word my ears tingled as if all the blood in my body had rushed up into them. Visitors! I felt sure they would be betrayers--they would be persons who either knew me, or the real cousin, and then good-by to my *incognito*--good-by to the secret interview! What would become of it when I had to take to flight?

'Visitors! How very tiresome,' exclaimed Hannè. The servant mentioned a name unknown to me; that, as it appeared, of a family in the neighbourhood. I was not acquainted with them--but the cousin, my other self ...

'Visitors!' I exclaimed, in dismay. 'Do I know them? Will anybody have the great kindness to tell me if they are acquainted with me?'

They all laughed, and assured me that I was not acquainted with them. It was a family who had only lately settled in the neighbourhood, having exchanged a property in Jutland for one in Zealand, and with whom they were themselves but slightly acquainted. I recovered my spirits, and we turned our steps back towards the house. Gustav seized the opportunity to make his escape, the Justitsraad made no effort to detain him, and I was too much occupied with my own affairs to trouble myself at that moment about those of other people. The poor dear Jutland family had made a most unseasonable visit.

I thanked Heaven that I had never seen them before; and I cannot say that I should feel any regret at never beholding them more. They were a set of tiresome bores, who deprived me of the brightest afternoon of my life, and took the evening also; so that I had reason not to forget them in a hurry. My cousins had to amuse the silly daughters, the elder individuals on both sides discoursed together, and it fell to my share to entertain the son and his tutor. I looked a hundred times at my watch; I foretold that we were going to have thunder and lightning and rain in torrents--in short, I left no stone unturned to get rid of them early--but to no avail; I only reaped jeers and bantering from Hannè for my pains; and when at length they seemed themselves to think it expedient to go, she pressed them to stay longer, only to annoy me, and was mischievous enough to say, 'You surely will not refuse my cousin his first request to you,' thereby, as it were, making me pronounce my own doom. It was enough to put one into a rage.

We went to supper with all due formality, and for the first time I remembered that it was my duty to offer my arm to Jettè. She accompanied me like a lamb led to the sacrificial altar, and took the earliest opportunity of informing me that her headache had not yet left her. Headache is an absolute necessity for ladies; I do not know what they would do if no such thing as headache existed.

It was not possible to utter a word which could not be overheard by the tutor, who sat on the other side of her; at length it occurred to me to engage him in a conversation with Hannè, and with some difficulty I managed to do this. But fate had no compassion on me that evening. Presently I heard my real name pronounced by the father of the family who were visiting us; I felt as much shocked and alarmed as if he had shouted '*Seize that thief!*' I had nearly dropped my fork.

'He is a most respectable man, I can assure you; I recommend you to send all your corn to him; he is very fair in his dealings. I have known him for a long time.'

It was of my father he was speaking.

'I shall consider about it,' said the Justitsraad; 'I do not know the house myself. And he has a son, you say. Is the son a partner?'

'It was intended that he should be,' said my personal enemy; 'but he is such a sad scamp that I think the father will hardly venture to take him into partnership. He played such foolish, wild pranks at home, that he was sent to Hamburg; but he did not go on a bit better there, as I have heard.'

'I am sorry for the poor father,' said the Justitsraad.

'A good character is valuable,' thought I. 'Here is the second time to-day that my name has been stigmatized. Now, both my person and my name are contraband at ---- Court. Cruel fate!' I became quite silent--willingly would I also have taken refuge in a headache; there was enough to give me one, at any rate; and I took leave in the coldest and most distant manner of the party who had prolonged their visit on my account.

'Pray come and see us soon with your betrothed,' said the old wretch who had made so free with my town character.

It was with difficulty that I kept my temper, and poor Jettè seemed also to be on thorns.

'What nice people they are!' exclaimed Hannè; 'the daughters have promised me to come here at least twice a week. But you were quite silent and stupid this evening, cousin.'

'It was what you wished me to be in the morning,' I replied; 'I only conducted myself according to your desire.'

'Let me always find you so obedient. Goodnight! To-morrow I shall command you to be gay again. That becomes you best, after all.' She held out her pretty little hand as a token of reconciliation.

'And I beg of you to come into the grove to-morrow morning, after breakfast; I wish very much to have a little private conversation with you,' whispered Jettè, almost in tears, as I kissed her hand. She could hardly bring herself to pronounce the words; I saw what a pang it cost her. A warm pressure of her hand was my only reply; she little knew how friendly my feelings were towards her.

'So my adventures are not finished even with this day,' said I to myself as I opened a little of the window in my room; 'shall I make up my mind to this delay, or shall I take myself off at once! What! leave poor Jettè in the lurch? Yet how can I help her? What is the use of my remaining longer here?--I shall but entangle myself still more deeply in a net of untruth, which will bring me into disgrace. Have I not had warnings enough--the gallows scene, my Hamburg reputation, and the many uneasy moments I have passed to-day? I am vexed and annoyed this evening; it will cost me less, therefore, perhaps, to recover my freedom tonight than to-morrow night; another day with Hannè will only make me feel the separation still more acutely. Then, in case of a discovery, how shall I excuse this prolonged mystification? By confessing my love for Hannè?--a pretty apology, to be sure! But am I *really* in love with her? *I* in love! and if I were, what would be the result? Is it at all likely that the Justitsraad would give his daughter to an impertinent puppy, who had made her acquaintance first by such an unwarrantable trick--to a "sad scamp" who had only made himself remarkable by his wild pranks? Or--shall I climb up yon tree, perch myself like a singing-bird before Jettè's window, make my confession to her, and then start on my pedestrian journey? Or--shall I go to bed, and let to-morrow take care of itself? I will consult my buttons--I will try my fate by them. Let me see: I will ... I will not ... I will ... I will go to bed. ... Aha! I am to go to bed--chance has so decided it for me. But to go to bed in love! that such a catastrophe should happen to me! I had thought it was quite foreign to my nature; however, here I am, up to my ears in love. Ah! why was that little fairy, Hannè, so bewitching? why were the whole family so frank and pleasant? It was all their own fault; they forced the cousinship upon me. Heaven knows I came to them quite innocent of nefarious designs--fast asleep and snoring--perfectly honourable.... *Apropos* of honour, let me close the window; what Gustav and Jettè have to talk about is nothing to me--it would be very indelicate to play the listener--wounding to my better feelings. My better feelings! I can't help laughing at the idea of *my* being inconvenienced by any symptoms of honourable, or delicate, or *better* feelings. It is my cursed levity and folly that lead me astray; after all, there *are* honesty and uprightness in me, *au fond*, and my heart is in its right place. I will no longer be the slave of caprice and impulse. I will be something better than a mere madcap; and here, even here, they shall learn to speak of me with respect.... Ah! it will be a confounded long time, however, before I can teach them that ... and ... in the meantime, I positively am in love.'

Having arrived at this conclusion, I betook myself to my couch, and closed my eyes, at the same time burying my ears in my pillows, not to overhear any portion of the discourse which was to be carried on about one o'clock in the morning, on the outside of my window, and also the sooner to dream of Hannè. I succeeded in both, for I heard or saw nothing whatsoever of the two unfortunate lovers, and I dreamed of Hannè the livelong night. The morning was far advanced, when Thomas thrust his head into my room, and rated me for being as heavy a slumberer as one of the seven sleepers;--the little wretch! I was at that moment swinging with Hannè, and would have given the wealth of the East India Company to have been permitted to end my dream undisturbed.

When I entered the breakfast-room they were all at table. Jettè looked very pale, but she allowed that her headache was better, though she said she still felt far from well. Hannè and her father teased me unmercifully about the visitors of the day before, who had put me so much out of humour, and about my predictions of a thunderstorm wherewith I endeavoured to drive them away. 'But you are quite an ignoramus in regard to the weather, cousin; that I perceived,' said Hannè, 'I shall present you with a barometer on your birthday, so that you may not make such mistakes again as that of yesterday evening. Which is the important day?'

'It is quite old-fashioned to keep birthdays, Hannè; that custom has been long since exploded,' said I, 'and therefore I am not going to tell you.'

'But we are very old-fashioned here, and you will be expected to do as we do in respect to keeping birthdays. First, let me refresh your memory. When is my birthday?'

'On the 12th of November you will be seventeen years of age.'

'Right. And Jettè's? How old will she be her next birthday?'

It was a trying examination, but it was well deserved; why had I not taken myself off the night before, when I could so well have made my escape?

'Come, begin; tell us Jettè's birthday, and my father's, and my mother's? Let us have them all at once. Now we shall see whether you are skilled in your almanac.'

'Are you seriously bent on this examination? Do you fancy I have forgotten one of them?' I asked, in an offended tone. 'I will not answer such questions.'

This was one way of escaping. When do people most easily take offence? Answer: When they are in the wrong.

'I see how it is,' said Hannè; 'as it annoys you to be asked if you are betrothed, it probably annoys you to be expected to remember the birthday of her to whom you are engaged. Only think,' she added, addressing the rest of the party, 'he does not wear his betrothal-ring, because he does not like answering any question to which his having it on his finger might give rise. As if it were a question of conscience.'

'So it may be, sometimes,' I replied. 'But since questioning is the order of the day, I beg to ask why *you* wear that little ring on your finger?'

'I never gratify impertinent curiosity,' said the little devil, colouring up to the very roots of her hair. She seemed very much vexed, and turned angrily away.

'Now--now--children! can you never agree?' said the Justitsraad. 'You two will be getting into quarrels every moment, that I foresee; you resemble each other too much; it is from the absolute similarity between you that you cannot be in peace.'

'You flatter me very much, uncle,' said I; 'would that it were really so.'

'I say nothing of the kind,' cried Hannè; 'I beg to decline the compliment. Gentlemen full of whims are my aversion. But, happily for both of us, you are not engaged to me. Jettè is much too good--she will put up with your bad habits.'

Jettè smiled kindly to her, and that seemed immediately to appease her wrath. She ran to her sister, kissed her, and said, 'For your sake I will bear with him; but believe me, you will not make an endurable husband of him if you do not begin in time to drive his caprices out of him. He should be accustomed to do as he is bid, and answer the questions that are put to him.'

Both Jettè and myself turned our faces away to conceal our confusion. Hannè held out her hand to me. 'Do you repent of your sins?'

'With my whole heart.'

'Will you beg pardon, and promise henceforth to be better?'

'Yes. I confess that I am a great sinner, but I humbly beg pardon, and will try to do better for the future.' So saying, I pressed a long, long kiss on her hand; I could hardly get my lips away from it.

'So--that is enough. Now go and beg Jettè's pardon, because you have been naughty in her presence; and,' she added, 'kiss her hand prettily.'

I did so.

'Very well. But I don't think you have ever kissed her as your betrothed yet. Let me see you go through that ceremony, properly too.'

Poor Jettè became crimson at this challenge, which did not in the least embarrass me.

I felt that it was going a little too far, but what could I do? Dear reader, I was compelled to kiss the young lady--do not judge of me too severely because I did it. But I obeyed the command in as formal a manner as possible; it was scarcely a kiss, yet it burned on my lips like fire; as to how it burned my conscience--well, I will say nothing of that.

'He is really quite timid,' exclaimed Hannè, who stood by with her hands folded, watching the performance of her command; 'I did not expect such an assured young gentleman to be so ceremonious; one would think it were his first essay!'

'And peace being now restored and sealed,' said the Justitsraad, 'I hope it will be a Christian, a universal, and an eternal peace, both for the present and the future; that is to say, at least till you fall out again. And in order that such may not be the case for a few hours, we will leave the ladies, nephew, and pay a visit to the new horse I bought the other day. We shall see if you are as good a judge of horses as you are of the Hamburg theatricals.'

'You really should give poor Carl some peace,' said my considerate aunt, 'you will make him quite tired of us all. One insists upon catechizing him as to dates, another as to his veterinary knowledge--there is only wanting that I should attack him about culinary lore. You shall not be so plagued by them, Carl: as to the horse it was my husband's own choosing; and if you should not instantly discover, by looking at its teeth, that it is young and handsome, and has every possible good quality, you will be called an ignoramus.'

'Any how he may be called that,' said Hannè; 'but I forgot, peace has been proclaimed, so let my words be considered as unspoken.'

PART III

About an hour before luncheon I stole away into the wood to wait for Jettè, and it was with a beating heart I listened for any approaching footsteps; had I not kissed her, I should have felt easier in my own mind. Ought I now to confess to her the impositions of which I had been guilty? Perhaps it would be better to do so ... But the kiss ... would she forgive that?

I discerned her white dress a good way off, and I almost felt inclined to hide myself, and let her take the trouble of finding me; but again I bethought me that it was not the part of the cavalier to be shamefaced in a secret assignation. I therefore went forward to meet her. As soon as she caught a glimpse of me, she stopped, and suddenly changed colour. The poor girl--how sorry I was for her! She could not utter one word. I led her to a rural seat near.

'Cousin,' at length she said, 'it must doubtless surprise you, and naturally so too, that I should in such a secret manner have requested an interview with you. If you could conceive how painful this moment is to me, I am sure you would compassionate me.'

'My dear young lady, I owe you an explanation, and I thank you for having given me an opportunity ...'

'Dear cousin, be not offended with me--do not speak to me in that distant and ceremonious manner--it makes the step more painful which I am about to take, and which cannot be longer delayed. It is I who owe you an explanation--alas! an explanation that will deprive me of your esteem and your friendship. I am very unhappy.'

'Do not weep so, dear cousin; you cannot imagine how it grieves me to see you so miserable. Believe me, I have your happiness sincerely at heart. You little know what delight it would give me if I were able to say to myself that I had contributed to it.'

The double signification which my words might bear drew forth more tears. Jettè cried, without making any reply.

'There is comfort for every affliction,' I continued. 'God has mercifully placed the antidote alongside of the poisonous plant. Tell me, at least, what distresses you--let me at least endeavour to console you, even if I cannot assist you, and do not doubt my good will, though my power may be but limited.'

'For Heaven's sake, Carl, do not speak so kindly to me,' cried Jettè, with some impetuosity. 'Do not speak thus--I have not deserved it. If you would be compassionate, say that you hate me--that you abhor me.'

'And if I said so, I should only deceive you. No, Jettè, my complaisance cannot go so far.'

'You would hate me--you would despise me!' she exclaimed, sobbing, 'if you only knew ... oh! I shall never be able to tell ... if you only knew ... how unfortunate I am ... how I ...'

'Dear Jettè,' said I, in some agitation, 'you have come to enter into an explanation with me; allow me to assist your confession, and help to lighten the burden which weighs so heavily on your heart. You have come, I know, to break off with me.'

'*You know!*' she exclaimed, in consternation. And she seemed as if she were going to faint. 'Take pity on me, Carl; leave me for a few minutes; I dare not look you in the face.'

She buried her own face in her pocket-handkerchief, and wept bitterly. I kissed her hand, and left her.

Very much out of spirits myself, I wandered to and fro under the trees.

'How is all this to end?' said I to myself; 'the poor girl will fret herself to death if she cannot have her Gustav, and get rid of her cousin. Gustav is a fine fellow, and a very good match; even the father allows that. The cousin must be an idiot to let himself be betrothed by his father's orders to a girl he knows nothing about--and a tiresome one too, according to what is reported of him. Jettè is a girl with a great deal of feeling--but he must be a clod with none; he can't care in the least for her, or he would have been here long ere this. He shall not have her. What, if I were to advise them to run away an hour or two before I take myself off? or, suppose we were all three to elope together? Nonsense! How can I think of such folly? Poor girl it would melt a heart of stone to see her crying there. What if I were to stay and play the cousin a little longer--formally renounce her hand--give her up to Gustav? I should like to act such a magnanimous part ... and when it was all well over, and the real cousin arrived, to let him find that he had come on a fool's errand, and go back to nurse his cold ... or, it might be better to drop him a line by the post to save a scene? I'll do it. By Jove! I'll do it The god of love himself must have sent me here; no man in the wide world could do the thing better than myself. But what right have I to decide thus the fate of another man--a man whom I have never even beheld? Right! It is time to talk about *right*, forsooth, after I have been doing nothing but wrong for thirty-six hours. No, no, let conscience stand to one side, for the present at least; it has no business in this affair. I have acted most unwarrantably, I know, but I will make up for my misdeeds by one good deed--one blessing will I take with me; and when I am gone, two happy persons at least will remember me kindly, and Hannè will be less harsh in her judgment of my conduct, since it will have brought about her sister's happiness. Let me set my shoulders to the wheel--there is no time to lose. No, they shall not all execrate me.'

Jettè was still sitting on the bench where I had left her. I placed myself beside her, and tried to reassure her.

'I said I owed you some explanation; allow me in a few words to tell you all you wish to communicate. You do not care for me--you love Gustav Holm--you will be wretched if you cannot find some good pretext for breaking off the match with me--you have many reasons to love him, none to love me--you want to let me know how the matter stands, and to give me a basket,[4] but to do it in so amicable a manner, that you hope I will accept it quietly like a good Christian, and not make too much fuss about it. All this is what you would have told me sooner or later. Am I not right, Jettè? or is there more you would have entrusted to me?'

She hid her face with her hands.

'My window was partly open the other night,' I added. 'I overheard your conversation with Gustav Holm, and I knew immediately, of course, what I had to expect. You will believe, I hope, that I have sufficient feeling not to wish to force myself upon one who cannot care for me. Forgive me that I have caused you any uneasiness; it was against my own will. I would much rather have convinced you sooner that you have no enemy in me, but, on the contrary, a sincere friend.'

'Dearest, best Carl! Noblest of men! You restore me to freedom--you restore me to life! The Almighty has heard my prayers! You do not know how earnestly I have prayed that you might find me detestable.'

'Therein your prayers have not been heard, Jettè,' said I. 'If you could have loved me, I could not have wished a better fate. I love you and Hannè much more than you think.' I felt that every word I had just spoken was positive truth. Jettè wrung my hand.

'You have removed a mountain from my heart,' she replied. 'Would that I could thank you as you deserve!'

I was quite ashamed of all the thanks she poured out, and all the gratitude she expressed. It is an unspeakable pleasure to promote the happiness of one's fellow-creatures; it is an agreeable feeling which I would not exchange for any other.

When the first burst of joy was over, Jettè consulted with me how it would be best to break the matter to her father. I told her of his good opinion of Gustav, and built upon it the brightest hopes.

Jettè shook her head. 'He will insist that I shall keep my promise,' said she, mournfully. 'He will not relinquish a plan which he has cherished for so many years. How dreadful it is for me to disappoint him!'

'Very well, take me.'

'Oh! do not jest with me, dear Carl. My only dependence is on you.'

'I shall take my departure immediately, and leave a letter renouncing my engagement to you. That will go far to help you.'

'For Heaven's sake, stay! You are the only one who can speak to him,' said she. 'You have already acquired much influence over him.'

'Then let us proceed at once to the *éclaircissement*. I shall tell him that I have discovered that your heart belongs to Gustav Holm, not to me; and that I cannot accept any woman's hand unless her heart accompanies it.'

'Oh! what a terrible moment it will be when that is said! I tremble at the very idea of it. You do not know what he can be when his anger is thoroughly roused.'

'Then would you prefer to elope with Gustav? Like a loyal cousin, I will assist you in your escape.'

'That would enrage him still more; he has always been so kind and gentle to me.'

'I wish we had Gustav here, that something might be determined on. These anticipated terrible moments are never so dreadful in reality as in expectation; you have had a proof of this in the one you have just gone through.'

'Gustav will be here soon; he knows that I had requested this private conversation with you ... he will meet me here in the wood ... he will come when--when....' She stopped, and blushed deeply.

'He will come when I am gone,' I said, laughing. 'That was very sensibly arranged, but the arrangement must be annulled nevertheless, and he must make the effort of showing himself while I am here. I dare say he is not many miles off--perhaps within hail. Mr. Holm! Mr. Holm!' I roared at the top of my voice. 'He knows my manner of inviting him, and you will see that he will speedily present himself. Good morning, Mr. Holm!' I added.

'For God's sake do not shout so loudly, you will be overheard,' said Jettè. 'Oh! how will all this end?'

'Uncommonly well,' thought I. 'Here comes the lover.'

Gustav came, almost rushing up; his countenance and manner expressed what was passing in his mind, namely, uncertainty whether he was to look on me as a friend or a foe.

'Gustav--Carl!...' exclaimed Jettè, sinking back on the bench. She found it impossible to command her voice; but her eyes, which dwelt with affection on us both, filled up the pause, and expressed what words would not.

I took his hand and led him up to Jettè. He knelt at her feet, she threw her arms round his neck, while I bent over them, and beheld my work with sincere satisfaction. There was a rustling in the bushes, and Hannè and her father stood suddenly before us! The lovers did not observe them, although I did my utmost by signs to rouse their attention.

'What the devil is all this?' exclaimed the Justitsraad, in a voice of thunder. 'What does this mean? Carl, what are you doing?'

'I am bestowing my cousinly benediction and full absolution and remission of sins, as you ought to do, my worthy uncle,' I replied, as cheerfully as I possibly could. It was necessary to appear to keep up one's courage. Gustav rose hastily, and Jettè threw herself into her sister's arms.

'My dear sir!' said Gustav, imploringly.

'Mr. Holm!' cried the Justitsraad, drawing himself up.

'Dear uncle!' I exclaimed, interrupting them both, 'allow me to speak. Gustav adores Jettè, and she returns his love. There can be no more question about me; I am her cousin, and nothing either more or less. I am not such an idiot as to wish to force a woman to be my wife whose heart is given to another. I have dissolved the engagement between Jettè and myself, deliberately, and after due reflection. I *could* not make her happy, and I *will not* make her unhappy. There stands the bridegroom, who only awaits your blessing. Give it, dear uncle, and let this day become the happiest of my life, for it is the first time I ever had an opportunity of doing good.'

'Heavens and earth! a pretty piece of work, indeed!' The Justitsraad was as blustering as a German, and would on no account allow himself to hear reason. A great deal of his anger was naturally directed against me. I tried to smooth matters down. Jettè wept and sobbed. It was a hundred to one against us. 'I shall write to your father this very day,' he said, at length; 'he only can absolve me from my vow; but that he will not do--that he certainly will not do on any account. This marriage has been his greatest wish, for I do not know how many years, as well as mine.'

'But he will be obliged to do it,' said I; 'this very afternoon I shall take my departure, and you shall never hear of me more. My father's power over me by no means extends so far as you seem to fancy. I will not make Jettè miserable, merely to indulge his whims. Dear uncle, let me persuade you to believe that your contract is null and void: give your blessing to Gustav and Jettè, and leave me to settle the matter with my father. Feelings cannot be forced. Jettè does not care for me, and you ought not, in this affair, to be less liberal than I am.'

'Liberal--liberal indeed! He is always prating about such folly,' exclaimed the Justitsraad, in a rage. 'It is that abominable Berlin liberality that has entirely ruined him.'

Berlin liberality! It was the first time I had ever heard *that* bewailed. But what absurd things do people not stumble upon when they are angry, and speak without reflection.

'Well, it was Berlin that ruined me, according to my uncle, and so utterly ruined me ... that I am betrothed in Berlin, and cannot be betrothed again. It is against the law both here and in Prussia to have two wives.'

This was an inspiration prompted by the exigency of the occasion; what did one untruth more or less signify? I was a Jesuit at that moment, and excused myself with Loyola's doctrine--that the motive sanctifies the means.

'Betrothed!' exclaimed the Justitsraad--'betrothed in Berlin! Make a fool of me! Hark ye, Carl ...'

'Betrothed!' interrupted Hannè. 'Upon my word, you are a fine fellow, cousin. That is the reason he does not wear Jettè's betrothal-ring. And I to be standing here admiring his magnanimity!'

Jettè silently held out her hand to me from one side, Gustav from the other; these were well-meant congratulations.

'Yes, betrothed,' I continued. 'Abuse me at your will, hate me, curse me, say and do what you please, but betrothed I am, and betrothed I must remain.'

This was a settler. The wrath of the Justitsraad cooled by degrees; that really kind-hearted man could not withstand so many anxious looks and earnest prayers; and fear of all the gossip and ridicule to which his holding out longer under the circumstances might give rise, also had effect upon him.

'You are a sad scapegrace, Carl,' he said, 'and Jettè may be thankful she is not to have you for her husband; but she shall not be left in the lurch on account of your foolish freaks.' He took her hand and placed it in Gustav's, saying, 'You must make up to me for the failure of those hopes which I have cherished through so many years. But,' he added, with a sigh, 'what will my brother say when he hears this history?'

Jettè cast herself upon his neck; she almost fainted in his arms; the rest of us surrounded him. There was no end to embraces and thanks.

'And now let us hasten to my mother,' said Hannè; 'the revolution shall end there. I would not be in your place, cousin, for any money; you will be soundly rated.'

'You shall be my advocate, Hannè, and shall defend my case; it is only under your protection that I dare appear before my aunt. Take me under your wing--I positively will not leave you.'

I slipped my arm round her waist, and I think, if I remember aright, I was going to kiss her.

'Hands off, Mr. Cousin! Now that you are not to be my brother-in-law you must not make so free. Remember your intended in Berlin.'

Alas! to help others I had injured myself. Hannè, her father, and I walked on first, the lovers followed us a little way behind. As we came along we met some of the peasantry on the estate going to their work.

'Hollo! good people!' cried I to them, 'this evening we must be all merry, and drink your master's good health, and dance on Miss Jettè's betrothal-day. Hurrah for Miss Jettè and Mr. Holm!'

'Hurrah!' cried the people. And the declaration was made.

'Be quiet, you good-for-nothing!' cried the Justitsraad, 'and don't turn everything topsy-turvy in a place that does not belong to you. A feast, forsooth--drink my health, indeed! It is easy for you to be generous at another's man's expense. I declare the fellow is determined to take the whip-hand of us all.'

My aunt heard the noise, and came out on the steps to ask what was the matter. I crept behind Hannè and hid myself.

'A complete revolution, my dear, which that precious fellow Carl has brought about. When the luncheon-bell had rung for some time in vain, without their making their appearance, Hannè and I went to look for Jettè and Carl in the wood; I expected to have found him at Jettè's feet; but instead of him there lay another, and he was actually busying himself in making up a match between them. Truly, it is an edifying story. Come in, and I will tell you all about it, and you will see to what purpose he has travelled. He has betrothed himself in Berlin, fancy--and very probably in Hamburg, in Paris, in Vienna, wherever he may have been. He is a fine fellow! A pretty viper we were nourishing in our hearts!'

My aunt was easily reconciled to the course of events, and she gave the young couple her maternal blessing. But it was me whom they all wanted for a son-in-law and a brother-in-law. It was very flattering to be such a favourite; however, as I was not to be had, they received Gustav (for whom they had a great regard) with open arms. We all became as sprightly as a parcel of children, and I would have been very happy had not the many affectionate good wishes for the future welfare of myself and my unknown *fiancée* in Berlin fallen like burning drops of molten lead on my soul, and had I not had constantly before me the remembrance that I must soon leave this pleasant circle, and for ever! My proposition to spend that day entirely by ourselves was agreed to, and orders were given to admit no visitors.

'Let me but live this day undisturbed to the end,' thought I, 'and I shall demand nothing more from Fortune, which has hitherto been so kind to me.' It was a day, the like of which I have never spent. You will, perhaps, think it strange, dear reader, that my conscience should be so much at ease; but I must frankly confess that the good action I had accomplished, and the happiness I had bestowed, had entirely had the effect of quieting that internal monitor. Jettè was right when she said that I had already obtained some influence over her father; for I can positively assert that my sudden and public announcement of the state of affairs had been taken in good part. I was all activity and excitement; and my exuberant mirth, which was almost without bounds, did not permit a serious word, scarcely a serious thought. I obliged them all to exert themselves, and fly about in order to make preparations for a little dance in a round summer-house at one end of the garden: the Justitsraad had to send to the village for two fiddlers; his wife had to give out sheets and curtains to make hangings for the walls; the young ladies wove garlands; Gustav and I manufactured chandeliers out of barrel-hoops and vegetables. Everybody was set to work, and before the evening the prettiest little ball-room that could be was arranged; and the people on the estate declared they had never seen anything so splendid before; 'but, to be sure, there had never been a betrothal feast in the family before.'

'You are a clever fellow, Carl,' said the Justitsraad; 'you have got this up so prettily and so well, that one might almost give a real ball. Were it not that I should have my wife and children up in arms against me, I really fancy I should like a dance. But there would be too many difficulties in the way.'

Hannè flew up to her father, and hugged him in her joy; he was taken at his word, and nothing else was talked of but the ball, which in the course of eight days was to be given to celebrate Jettè's betrothal.

'We will set about writing the invitations at once,' said Hannè; 'there is an hour or more yet before the people are to begin to dance, and we have nothing to do. Let us fetch pen, ink, and paper; I will dictate, and Carl shall write; it will be done directly, almost, and early to-morrow morning we shall send off the invitations. So, all the difficulties are overcome. Now, cousin, mend your pen; you write a good hand,' said Hannè.

'Write! No, that I won't,' thought I. 'I shall take good care not to betray myself by that.'

'Gustav can write what you want; I have hurt my hand,' said I, looking round; but Gustav and Jettè had both disappeared.

'How? Let me see,' said Hannè. 'It is not true. Gustav and Jettè have gone into the garden; we must let them alone; so you shall come, and you may as well do it at once.'

'But I have really hurt my finger, Hannè; it is extremely painful. I shall not be able to make the most wretched pothooks--my finger is quite swollen.'

'Or rather you are extremely lazy, and won't take the trouble,' said Hannè. 'But at least you shall help me to write a list of the people to be invited, before I forget half of them; I have got them all in my head just now, and your pothooks are good enough for that. Begin now! Put down first our neighbours who were here yesterday. Kammerraad[5] Tvede, with his wife, his two daughters, his son, and the tutor. Have you got them down?' Hannè looked over my shoulder at the paper. 'But what in the world stands there?' she asked.

'Kammerraad Tvede, with his wife, his two daughters, his son, and the tutor,' I replied. 'These are Greek characters, Hannè; I can write nothing but Greek with this finger.'

'But I can't read Greek, you refractory monster!' cried Hannè, dolefully.

'You must learn it, then, Hannè. Task for task; if you force me to write the list, I will force you to read Greek.'

'That's right, my boy!' exclaimed the Justitsraad, laughing heartily. 'If one gives the girls an inch, they are sure to take an ell; they would take the command of us altogether, if they could.'

After a great deal of joking and foolery, we accomplished making out the list, and the last name given was that of my good uncle, the worthy pastor, whom it was my purpose to visit, and whose guest I would be before the sun rose on the following day.

'Do you know him, too?' I asked, with a feeling of mingled surprise and annoyance.

'He confirmed both Jettè and me,' said Hannè; 'he is an excellent man, therefore I kept him to the last. You can hardly imagine how much we are all attached to him. If ever I marry, he shall perform the ceremony, I think you must remember him; at least, you saw him in this house more than once when you were here as a child.'

'Very true. I think I recollect him; he is a tall, old man, with a hooked nose. Yes, I remember him distinctly.'

This time, at least, I had no need to help myself out with lies! In a situation such as mine, one seizes with avidity every opportunity to speak truth; it is so very refreshing when one is up to the ears in untruth.

Our chandeliers answered their purpose exceedingly well: the fiddlers scraped loudly and merrily, and the floor shook under the powerful springs and somewhat weighty footing of the country swains and damsels who were dancing in honour of Miss Jettè's betrothal. I had taken a turn in the waltz with each of the village belles, and danced that furious *Fangedands* with Hannè--a dance that one must have seen the peasantry execute, in order to form an idea how violent it is. Glee and good-humour reigned around, and even the Justitsraad entered heartily into the joyous spirit which seemed to prevail. And, although from time to time, he whispered to me, 'I ought to be very angry at you--you have played me a pretty trick,' yet he was not in the slightest degree angry; on the contrary, he submitted with an extremely good grace to what he could not help. But I--I who had been the originator and cause of all this gaiety and gladness--I felt only profound melancholy, and stole away to indulge in it amidst the most lonely walks of the garden, or in the wood beyond. The hour of my departure was drawing rapidly near.

Perhaps you may imagine, dear reader, that it would be impossible for me to be sad or serious. Could you have beheld me wandering about the grounds alone, that September evening, when every one else was dancing, you would have found that you were mistaken in your opinion of me. I ascended the sloping hill, on which stands Hannè's favourite swing. By day the view from thence is beautiful; and even at night it is a place not to be despised. The garden, stretching out darkly immediately beneath, looked like an impenetrable wood. The moon was in its first quarter, and therefore shed but a faint uncertain light over objects at a little distance, while its trembling rays fell more brightly on the far-off waves of the Baltic Sea, making them appear nearer than they really were. On the right, the walls and chimneys of the dwelling-house gleamed through the openings of the trees; on the left, light blazed from the illuminated summer-house, whence came the sound of a hundred feet, tramping in time to the overpowered music. All else was as still around me as it generally is in the evening in the country, where the occasional bark of some distant dog, with its echo resounding from the wood, is the only sign of life. Behind me lay the pretty grove; and above my head stood the swing, on one of whose tall supporters my name was fastened in derision.

Had you seen how carefully I detached the piece of paper from the wood, and placing myself in the swing where I had sat with Hannè, allowed myself to rock gently backwards and forwards, while I gazed on the strange name that had become dearer to me than my own, because *she* had pronounced it and written it, you would have perceived that I also could have my sad and serious moments. But people of my temperament seek to avoid observation when a fit of blue-devils seizes them, and only go forth among their fellow-beings when the fit has subsided.

Jettè and Gustav took me by surprise. They had passed in silence through the garden, and arm-in-arm they had as silently ascended the little eminence.

'What, you here! in solitude, and so serious, dear cousin?' said Jettè; 'you look quite out of spirits. Everyone connected with me should be happy on this my betrothal day, and I must reckon you among the nearest of those--you, whom I have to thank for my happiness. Come and take a share in the joy you have created; if I did not know better, I might be inclined to fancy that you are grieving over the irreparable loss you have had in me: you really do assume such a miserable countenance.'

'Do not ridicule me, Jettè; I have perhaps just lost more than I can ever be compensated for.'

'It is well that a certain person in Berlin cannot overhear what politeness induces you to say in Zealand,' replied Jettè. 'But a truce to compliments at present, they only cast a shade of doubt over your truthfulness: keep them for those who know less of your affairs than I do, and let us speak honestly to each other. In reality, you are glad not to become more nearly connected with us than you are already: you cannot deny that.'

'Do you think so? And if that were far from the fact?--if, on the contrary, that were the cause of my melancholy--the knowledge of the impossibility of my being so--what would you say?'

'I should be under the necessity of pitying you very much, poor fellow!' said Jettè, laughing. 'But who would have thought that this morning?'

'You may indeed pity me, Jettè, for when I leave this place my heart and my thoughts will remain behind, with you--with all your dear family; and I must leave you soon.'

'Soon! Are you going abroad again?' asked Gustav.

'Two days after your arrival among us!' exclaimed Jettè; 'no, no, we cannot agree to that.'

'And yet it must be,' I said. 'I shall be gone, perhaps, sooner than you think. I have my own peculiar manner of coming and going, and ...'

'But what whim is this, Carl?' asked Jettè, interrupting me. 'Did you not come to spend some time with us? You may depend on it my father will not hear of your going, though our wishes and requests may have no influence over you.'

'I am compelled to go, dear Jettè; I must leave you for some time. Perhaps we shall meet again ... but should that be impossible, I shall write you, if you will permit me. And when I am gone, will you take my part, if I should be made the subject of animadversion? Let me hope, dear Jettè, that you and Gustav will think kindly of me, and that on the anniversary of this day you will not forget me when you stroll together through that wood which was this morning the scene of my dismissal.'

They both shook hands with me.

'But Carl, I hardly understand you,' said Jettè; 'you are so grave, so strange; you speak as if we were about to part for ever. Have you any idea of settling in Berlin?'

'I beseech you, Jettè, speak not of Berlin--that was a subterfuge, a story, which came suddenly into my mind; I could not pitch upon any better excuse wherewith to upset your father's plan in a hurry, or I would not have lied against myself. I assure you I have never put my foot in Berlin, nor am I betrothed to anyone.'

Jettè stepped back a few paces, and fixed on me a look of surprise and earnest inquiry.

'What!' she exclaimed, 'you have never been at Berlin? You have told what is not true about yourself to help me? You are not engaged?'

'No; as certainly as that I stand at this moment in your presence, I am not engaged, and have never attempted to become so. I have only put myself in the way of receiving one refusal in my life,' I added, smiling, as Jettè began to look suspiciously at me, 'and that was this morning in yonder wood. Were it not superfluous, I could with ease give you the most minute particulars.'

There was a short silence; then Jettè exclaimed,

'You are a noble creature, Carl; may God reward you, for I cannot. But day and night I will pray for your welfare.' She was much affected, her voice faltered. Gustav shook my hand cordially.

'My dear friends,' said I, 'do not accord to me more praise than I deserve, for the higher one is praised the greater is the fall when opinions change. Hear me before you promise to pray for me, and let me tell you how ... but no, no, let me keep silence--let me say nothing. Pardon my seeming caprice. Promise me that you will be my sincere and unshaken friends, and let us go and dance again. May I have the honour of engaging the bride for the next waltz?'

I had been on the point of confessing all my foolish pranks, and how I was imposing on them; but false shame prevented me. Was it better or not? I scarcely knew myself. I begged them to accompany me back to the summer-house. In the alley of pine-trees which led to it we met Hannè, who, according to her own account, was looking about for us; she almost ran against us before she perceived us.

'But, good Heavens I have you all become deaf? I have been calling you over and over, without receiving the slightest answer, and now I find you gliding about in deep silence, like ghosts, scaring people's lives out of them. I suppose Carl has been amusing himself, as usual, with mischief, and has been haunting you two poor lovers, and disturbing you. Do you not know, Carl, that you have no sort of business to be--in short, are quite an incumbrance where Jettè and Holm are? Now answer me--do you know this, or do you not, Carl?'

'No,' I replied, shortly.

'"*No!*" Is that a fitting answer to a lady? Be so good as to reply politely. I must take upon myself to teach you good manners before you go abroad again, else we shall have reason to be ashamed of you.'

And then she began to hum the song of 'Die Wiener in Berlin:'

'In Berlin, sagt er,
Musz du fein, sagt er,
Und gescheut, sagt er,
Immer sein, sagt er....'

'I wish Berlin were at the devil, Hannè!' I exclaimed, interrupting her; 'that is my most earnest desire, believe me.'

'A very Christian wish, and expressed in choicely elegant phraseology, everyone must admit.'

'Only think, Hannè, he has *never* been at Berlin, and is *not* betrothed there. Carl only made these assertions because he could think of no other way of making my father agree to our wishes,' said Jettè, almost crying.

'What! he is not engaged? He has never been in Berlin? Well! he is the greatest story-teller I ever met. Did he not stand up, and make positive declarations of these events, with the most cool audacity? It is too bad. Lying is the worst of all faults--it is the root of all evil.'

'No, my little Hannè, idleness is the root of all evil.'

'I dare say you abound in that root too. But I don't think you can ever have studied the early lesson-books, from which all children should be instructed. I shall myself hear you your catechism to-morrow, and rehearse to you the first principles of right and wrong; so that when you leave us, you may be a little better acquainted with the doctrines of Christianity than you are at present.'

'But he leaves us to-morrow, Hannè; he has assured us of that.'

'We positively will not allow him to make his escape,' said Hannè. 'At night we shall lock him in his room, and during the day Thomas shall watch him. That boy sticks as fast as a burr,--he won't easily shake him off.'

'But suppose I were to get out by the window? You cannot well fasten that on the outside.'

'And break your neck, forsooth. No, no; that way of making your exit won't answer.'

'Oh, people can climb up much higher than my window, and descend again without breaking their necks,' said I.

Jettè and Gustav coloured violently.

'Well, we can discuss that point to-morrow. This evening, at least, you will remain with us, on account of its being Jettè's betrothal day. Come, give me your arm, and let us take a walk; it is charming, yonder in the garden--within the summer-house one is like to faint from the heat.'

We strolled on, two and two, in the sweet moonlight; sometimes each pair sauntering at a little distance from the other--Hannè and I chatting busily, while Gustav and Jettè often walked in the silence of a happiness too new and too deep for the language of every-day life.

'Is it really true that you are going to leave us?' asked Hannè.

'It is, indeed, too true; I must quit this place.'

'Why? if I may venture to ask. But do not tell me any untruth.'

'Because I have been here too long already--because a longer residence among you all ... near you, dear Hannè, would but destroy my peace.'

'I expressly desired you not to tell me any lies. Good Heavens! is it impossible for you to speak truth two minutes together?'

'And is it impossible for you to speak seriously for two minutes together? What I have just said is the honest truth.'

'Humph! However, tell me, is it true or not true that you are engaged in Berlin? Who have you hoaxed--Jettè and me, or my father and mother? I beseech you speak truth this once.'

'If any one is hoaxed, it is your father, Hannè; but at the moment I could think of nothing else to shake his determination, or I certainly should not have composed such a story, for telling which I blamed myself severely.'

'Oh, of course I believe you! To make a fool of one's own excellent uncle! It is a sin that ought to lie very heavy on your conscience, Carl. It is almost as great a sin as to make fools of one's cousins.'

'That is a sin from which I hope you will absolve me. Ah, Hannè! what has most distressed me was, that my character must have appeared dubious in your eyes. From the first moment I was wretched, because I could not tell you that it was only a pretended engagement.'

'I do not see what *I* have to do with your being betrothed in Berlin or not. As far as I am concerned, you might be betrothed in China, if you liked.'

'Your gaiety of temper makes you take everything lightly, and yet it is you who have taught me that life has serious moments. You have transformed me, Hannè; if you could only know what an influence the first sight of you, the night I arrived here, has exercised upon my fate ...'

'Indeed! Do tell me all about it; what was the wondrous and fearful effect of the sight of me?' said Hannè, laughing.

'Dear Hannè, without intending it, you have pitched upon the right words, in calling it "wondrous and fearful." Yes, it will follow me like a heavy sentence from a judgment-seat, ever reproaching me with my thoughtlessness. Awake, and in dreams, will I implore forgiveness; I will kneel and pray for it. Look at me once more with that captivating glance which, yon evening, made me forget myself, and tell me that you will not hate me--loathe me--despise me: see, upon my knee I entreat one kind look--one kind word!'

I had actually fallen on one knee before Hannè, and had seized her hand--

'Let my hand go, you are squeezing it, so that you quite hurt me. That is not at all necessary to the part you are acting. Get up, cousin; you will have green marks on your knees, and I can't endure to see men in such an absurd, old-fashioned plight. You should be thankful that it is no longer the mode, when one is making love in earnest, to fall down on one's knees. These pastoral attitudes are very ridiculous; they savour of a shepherd's crook, and a frisky lamb with red ribbon round its neck.'

I arose quite crestfallen.

'At any rate I must allow that you promise to be a capital actor,' added Hannè. 'Next Christmas, when you come back, we shall get up some private theatricals: that will be charming! Last year we could not manage them, because we had no lover; Holm positively refused to act the part, unless I would undertake to be his sweetheart; and a play without love is like a ball without music.'

'Hannè, let us speak seriously for once. I really am going away, and shall be gone, perhaps, before you expect it; for I hate farewell scenes. It is not without emotion that I can think of leaving my amiable cousins, and God only knows if we shall ever meet again. Laugh at me if you will, I cannot forbid your doing that; but believe me when I tell you that your image will be present with me wherever I may go, and ...'

'You will travel in very good company, then,' said Hannè, interrupting me.

'Let me take the happy hope with me that I shall live in your friendly remembrance. Sink the cousin if you choose, dear Hannè; cousinship is not worth much, and let the term *friend* supersede it. That is a voluntary tie, for which I should have to thank but your own feelings. It is as a friend that I shall think of you when I go from this dear place, and as a friend that your image will follow me throughout the world.'

'Oh, it won't be very troublesome to you,' said Hannè. 'As to me, I don't happen to be in want of cousins, still less of friends. Let me see, in what office shall I instal you? Make a confidant of you? We do not employ any in our family; I am my own confidante: assuredly I could have none safer. I shall follow in this the example of my silent sister, who never gave me the slightest hint of her love for Gustav. A counsellor? Truly, such an accomplished fibber would make a trustworthy counsellor? No, I am afraid, if you throw up the post you hold, you will find it difficult to replace it by any other.'

'Very well, let me retain it then, but not as the gift of chance. You must yourself, of your own free will, bestow on me the title of your cousin, your chosen cousin: that is a distinction of which I shall be proud.'

'And will you, then, promise to come back at Christmas, and act plays with us?'

'I promise you into the bargain a summer representation, before autumn is over,' said I. 'The Fates only know if I shall preserve the dramatic talent I now have until winter.'

I had caught a portion of Hannè 's gaiety, and my sentimental feelings, so much jeered at, shrank into the background.

'Then I will dub you my cousin of cousins; and besides, on account of your many great services and merits, I will confer on you the distinguished title of my court story-teller.'

'And on the occasion of receiving this new title, I must, as in duty bound, kiss your hand; wherefore I remove this little brown glove, which henceforth shall be placed in my helmet, in token of my vassalage to a fair lady.'

'No, stop! give up my glove, cousin--I cannot waste it upon you. It is a good new glove, without a single hole in it. Give it up, I tell you; the other will be of no use without it.'

She tried to snatch it from me, but I held it high above her head, and speedily managed to seize its fellow-glove.

'You must redeem them, Hannè; a kiss for each of the pair is what I demand; and they are well worth it, for they are really nice new gloves. I will not part with them for less.'

'I think you must be a fool, Carl, to fancy for one moment that I would kiss you to recover my own gloves. No, I will die first,' she exclaimed, in a tone of comic indignation.

In answer to her mock heroics, I apostrophized the gloves in glowing terms, finishing with--'On your smooth perfumed surface I press my burning lips. Tell your fair mistress what I dare not say to her, what I at this moment confide to you.' I kissed the gloves.

'Well, well, give me back my gloves and I will let you kiss me,' said Hannè. 'But it shall be the slightest atom of a kiss, such as they give in the Christmas games, the most economical possible; it must not be worth more than four marks, for that was the price of the gloves. Now, are you not ashamed to take a kiss valued so low?'

'No, I will take it. But the value I put upon it is very different, for the slightest kiss from your lips, Hannè, is worth at least a million. You will make me a *millionnaire*, Hannè.'

I gave her the gloves, and was just on the point of kissing her, when the voice of the Justitsraad broke on the silence around, calling, 'Jettè, Hannè, Carl, hollo! where are you all?'

'Here,' cried Hannè, bursting away from me. 'We are coming.'

'But dearest, dearest Hannè! my kiss--my million?'

'We will see about it to-morrow; you must give me credit this evening.'

'My dearest Hannè, to-morrow will be too late; for Heaven's sake, have compassion on me! I am going away to-night; there is no to-morrow for me here. Give me but half the million now--but the quarter--but the four marks' worth which you owe me! Dear Hannè, pay me but the smallest mite of my promised treasure.'

'Nonsense! we must make the best of our way home, or we shall be well scolded.'

Gustav and Jettè joined us at that moment. The gloves and the kiss were for ever lost!

'Why, children, what has become of you, all this time?' exclaimed the Justitsraad. 'Come in now, and have a country-dance with the good folks before we leave them and go to have some mulled claret. Stop, stop, Carl, you can't dance with Hannè; she is engaged to one of the young farmers. You must take another partner. There is poor Annie, the lame milkmaid, she has scarcely danced at all; it is a sin that she is to sit all the evening, because one leg is a little shorter than the other. Go, dance with her.'

'Don't turn the poor girl's head with your enormous fibs,' cried Hannè to me, as I was entering the summer-house. 'Have pity on her unsophisticated heart, and do not speculate upon *a million there*; the herdsman would probably not allow it.'

'A million? The herdsman? What is all that stuff you are talking?' asked her father.

'Ill-nature--downright ill-nature, uncle.'

'Fie! cousin; that is not a chivalrous mode of speaking. But do go and foot it merrily with lame Annie, and I promise you the dance shall last at least an hour.'

The dance was over--the mulled wine was finished--the happy Gustav had gone to his home--the family had bid each other good night, and I was alone in my chamber.

'This was the last evening,' thought I to myself; 'the short dream was now over, and I had to leave that pleasant house, never more to return to it.' A deep sigh responded to these reflections. 'My deception will soon be discovered; they will revile and despise me. I shall most probably be the cause of their being exposed to the ridicule of the whole neighbourhood; that will annoy them terribly, and they will be very angry that anyone should have presumed to impose so impudently on their frank hospitality. And my kiss ... my million ... the realization of that delightful promise!... What if I were to remain yet another day--half a day--another morning even? Remain!--in order to add another link to the chain which binds me here, and which I am already almost too weak to sever? No--I will go hence. In about an hour the moon will set, and when its tell-tale light is gone I will go too. One short hour! Alas! how many melancholy hours shall I not have to endure when *that one* has passed. It is incomprehensible to me how I became involved in all this. Chance is sometimes a miraculous guide, when we allow ourselves to be blindly led by it. But a truce to these tiresome reflections; I have no time to think of anything but Hannè, now that I am about to leave her for ever ... *For ever!* These are two detestable words. Everything is now quite still in the house. I hear no sound but poor Pasop, rustling his chains in his kennel; he will not bark when he sees it is only I passing. They are all friendly to me here, even the very dogs; yet how false I have been to them!'

I threw my clothes and other little travelling appurtenances into my *valise*, and opened the window.

'But ought I to run away without leaving one word behind? The worthy family might be alarming themselves about me. What shall I write? I suppose I must play the cousin to the end; at any rate I must try to put them on a wrong scent. I shall address my note to Hannè, that she may see that my last thoughts were with her.'

I seized a pencil and wrote:--

'Hannè's cruelty has caused my bankruptcy and my flight. She could have made me a *millionnaire*, but she has left me a beggar. Poor and sad I quit this hospitable house, leaving behind my blessings on its much-respected and amiable inmates, including the hard-hearted fair one who has compelled me to seek a refuge at Fredericia, which, from the time of Axel, has afforded *jus asyli* to unfortunate subjects.'

I stuck the paper in the dressing-glass, where it would speedily be observed.

I had played out my comedy, and the sober realities of life were now before me. I fell into a deep reverie, which lasted until the first dawn of day, when I started up to prepare for my departure. First, I threw my carpet-bag out of the window, and then, getting out myself upon the tree, and cautiously descending from branch to branch, I reached the ground safely and quietly. Taking a circuitous route, I at length passed the woody village near my uncle's abode; and the sun stood high in the heavens when, weary and dispirited, and out of humour with the whole world, I entered the parsonage-house.

PART IV

Eight days after my arrival, I was sitting in the dusk with the old people, while my thoughts were at ---- Court. The good clergyman, according to habit, was shoving the skull-cap he wore on his head to and fro, and talking half-aloud to himself. At length he exclaimed,

'In good sooth, nephew, I am quite surprised at you. Is it natural for a young man to sit so much within doors? You have never gone a step beyond the garden and our little shrubbery, and really there is some very pretty scenery in our neighbourhood, quite worth your seeing.'

'It is a sin that he should be shut up here with us two old people,' said his wife; 'if our son had been at home, it would have been more pleasant for him. It is very unlucky that he should be at Kiel just now. How can we amuse such a young man, my dear? I am quite sorry for him.'

I assured them that I had everything I wished at their house, and was extremely comfortable. But the fact was, that I felt extremely uncomfortable. I was miserable at knowing that I was so near ---- Court, and yet could have no communication with its inhabitants; I was certain that I must have thrown everything there into the greatest commotion, yet, since my flight, I had heard nothing of or from the place round which my heart's dearest thoughts hovered continually.

'Why, instead of a wild, mischievous, merry madcap, as you were represented to be, we find a staid, quiet, grave young man. It is not a good sign when a gay temper takes such a sudden turn. You seem to be quite changed, nephew. Indeed, it strikes me your very appearance has altered; your hair looks darker to me, within these eight days, and your skin is as yellow as if you had the jaundice.'

'Oh, Heaven forbid! The Lord preserve him from that!' cried my worthy aunt, much alarmed.

I relieved her mind by assuring her that my health was excellent.

'And you are allowing the hair on your upper lip to grow to a pair of moustaches,' continued my uncle. 'You will soon look like an officer of hussars. If you were not such a sensible, quiet youth, I should think it was a piece of conceit and affectation, to look smart in the eyes of the girls.'

Without having formed any settled plan connected with the change of my appearance, but not without considerable trouble, had I by degrees blackened my hair, and darkened my complexion with walnut juice, so that I could not be recognized if any of the people from ---- Court should meet me. I had also cultivated moustaches for the same purpose, but they were as yet very diminutive.

'Just tell me, nephew, what do you want with moustaches?'

'I want them because ... I wish ... I must ... I belong to the corps of riflemen, uncle, and the new regulation is, that every rifleman is to have moustaches ... so I must mount a pair.'

'What a foolish regulation! Don't you think so, wife? But I suppose it is a case in which one must do as others do.'

This settled, I was left, as to my disguise, in peace. But my venerable uncle commenced another attack. 'I must positively have you to go out and look about you, Adolph. I am going to-morrow to see my friends Justitsraad ----, whose country seat is not far from this. You shall drive over there with me; the road is very pretty.'

I was in agony. 'I would, much rather remain at home, uncle; I don't know these people.'

'I will introduce you to them. They are a very amiable, charming family, and you will soon become acquainted with them. You absolutely must go.'

What excuse was I to manufacture? I had recourse to fibs again.

'The Justitsraad and my father are personal enemies--they quarrelled about some matter of business. They are deadly foes--I should be very unwelcome--my name is proscribed at ---- Court.'

'How very strange that I never heard of this before!' exclaimed the unsuspecting old man. 'People should not hate each other for the sake of sinful mammon. We must bring about a reconciliation between them. I shall certainly preach upon the subject of forgiveness next Sunday--a powerful discourse will I give.'

'It is also my wish that they should be reconciled, dear uncle, and therefore, I think it would be most prudent not to mention my name *yet*. If I make the acquaintance of the Justitsraad without his knowing who I am, I shall feel more at my ease with him. I assure you this will be best.'

'Well--so be it,' said my uncle; 'I will not then mention your being here. But I shall throw out a few hints about forgiveness and Christian feelings--these can do no harm.'

'No--that they cannot,' said my aunt. 'But I quite agree with Adolph. I think his plan a good one.'

As soon as the old people had retired to rest, I stole softly through the garden, and reaching the high road, took the way to ---- Court. As I approached it, I saw with pleasure the white summer-house on the outskirts of the garden. Soon after I reached the hill, where stood the well-known swing. The moon was shining brightly, and it was a lovely night. All was so still around, that I could hear the wind whistling through the adjacent alleys of trees--and the rustling of the wind amidst the branches of the pine and the fir has a peculiar sound. Far away in the wood was to be heard the melancholy tinkling of the bells worn by the sheep round their necks. There is a sadness in this monotonous, yet plaintive sound, which has a great effect upon the heart that is filled with longing--and where is the human being who has nothing to long for? But such sadness is not hopeless, and as the bells give tones sometimes higher, sometimes deeper, from different parts of the woods or fields, so tranquillizing voices whisper to our souls, 'There is comfort for every sorrow--we shall not always long in vain.'

The moon shed its soft light over the quiet garden, the clock struck eleven--that was generally the time at which the family retired to rest--therefore I ventured to leave my place of concealment, without the fear of encountering anyone. Presently after I stood again behind the bushes of fragrant jasmine, immediately beneath the windows, and beheld one light extinguished after the other. In the room I lately occupied, all was dark. At length the light also disappeared in Hannè's chamber.

Sleep, sweetly sleep! Dream blessed dreams!

I whispered with Baggesen, and my heart added, in the words of the same poet,

I love--I love--I love but only thee!

In Jettè's room there was still a candle burning; doubtless she was thinking of her Gustav, perhaps writing a few kind words to him. I could hardly refrain myself from climbing up *the* tree, and speaking to her; I had a claim upon her indulgence, for had I not laid the fountain of her happiness? *Laid the foundation!* How did I know that the real cousin had not arrived? But even in that case it would be scarcely possible to undo what had been done. I clung to the pleasing idea that I had effected some good.

At length Jettè's candle was extinguished also. The last--last light--I had gazed on it, till I was almost blinded. With an involuntary sigh I turned my steps slowly back towards the garden; something was moving close behind me; it was my quondam friend, a greyhound belonging to the Justitsraad, but he followed growling at my heels, as if he wished to hunt me off the grounds I polluted by my presence.

'Watchel! my boy! is that you? So--so--be still, be still, Watchel!' I turned to pat his head, but he showed his white teeth, and barked at me; and presently all the other dogs near began to bark also. 'Forgotten!' I exclaimed bitterly to myself, 'forgotten, and disliked!' Watchel followed me, snarling, to the extremity of the garden, and barked long at my shadow as I crossed the field.

The next day my uncle drove over to ---- Court. The moment he was gone I hurried up to his study, which looked towards the east, and arranged his large telescope to bear upon that place which had so much interest for me. I could overlook the whole plain; at its extremity was some rising ground studded with trees--this was the garden; to the left lay the grove, and close to it was the hillock on which stood the swing! Suddenly the swing, until then empty, seemed to be occupied with something white, which put it in motion. 'It is Hannè who is swinging!' I exclaimed aloud in my joy; and I spent the whole afternoon in gazing through the telescope, with a beating heart, and with my eyes fixed upon the swing to catch another glimpse of her who had vanished, alas! too soon. One glance at the folds of her white dress had thrown my blood into a tumult of excitement, but how wildly did not all my pulses beat when, towards evening, my uncle's carriage rolled up the avenue of the rectory.

After he had greeted my aunt with all due affection, and delivered the complimentary messages with which he was charged, inquired how things had gone on during the hours of his absence, settled himself comfortably in his old easy-chair, and lighted his pipe, he began with--

'I heard some very strange news over yonder; I really can think of nothing else.'

'What is it, dear? A great rise in the price of anything?' asked his wife.

'Oh no, my dear, not at all. It is a very ridiculous story. It is not to be mentioned; but I know you will keep it to yourself when I particularly request you to do so. Well--I will tell you all about it; it is really quite a mysterious affair.'

And the good man proceeded to relate how, one evening when they were expecting a cousin who was betrothed to Jettè, a person arrived who answered every question about the family, seemed to know all their affairs, gave himself out to be Carl, whom they had not seen for eleven years, and, as might be supposed, insinuated himself into the good graces of the whole of them. 'He found out that Jettè was attached to that young man Holm, who is studying agricultural affairs in this neighbourhood; so he insisted on annulling his engagement to her, declaring that he was not in love with her, but was betrothed abroad. The Justitsraad was at first very angry, but he gave way at last, and there were gay doings at ---- Court that evening. Next morning the cousin was nowhere to be found; but he left behind him a paper of which nobody can make anything. They expected him during two whole days, but he did not make his appearance again. On the third day, another person arrived, who also declared himself to be a cousin, said he was called Carl, and that he was the expected guest. He brought letters from his father, about whose handwriting there could be no doubt, and the whole family recognized him at once from many things. The first, of course, was an impostor. But Jettè is now betrothed to Holm as well as to the cousin, who had come to arrange about the wedding. There was an awful scene--he insisted on Holm's giving up Jettè to him, and her father had at last to interfere to prevent the rivals carrying their wrath to some fearful extremity. The cousin's obstinacy gave great offence, and he took his departure the day after he had arrived. But he was so angry, that it was with great difficulty he was induced to promise that he would hold his tongue, and not blab about this absurd affair.'

'May the Lord graciously preserve us all! It must have been some wicked sharper!' exclaimed my aunt, clasping her hands in great agitation, when her husband had finished his recital.

'Of course he was an impostor. But it is a very curious story. For what could he have come--will anyone tell me that?'

'Why, to steal, to be sure. Did he break into none of the keeping-places? Is there nothing missing--none of the plate? no forks or spoons?'

'Not the slightest article, and he was there for two days, and went about like one of themselves.'

'It is very surprising; but the fact is, he must have come to reconnoitre the premises, and, when the nights are longer and darker, they will hear of him again.'

'It is a most incomprehensible affair,' said I, in a voice that might have betrayed, me to more acute observers. 'And can they not guess at all who he is--have they no clue to him?'

'Not the slightest, nephew. They all describe him as a handsome, gentlemanly young man, who knew how to conduct himself in good society; and he acquitted himself so well in his assumed character, that none of them had the least notion what a trick he was playing them.'

'Believe me, my dear sirs, this person was no other than the celebrated Morten Frederichsen, who was arrested and imprisoned at Roeskilde, but made his escape. He must be a very clever fellow, that,' said my aunt; 'I have been told that he pretended to be a Russian officer once in Copenhagen, made his way into the higher circles, and spoke Russian as if it had been his mother tongue. No doubt he has contrived to get free again; and he is a dangerous man. Heaven preserve us from him! Where *he* is, there is always mischief going on. I will take care to see that the house-doors are well bolted and secured, and I shall tell the servants to let Sultan loose at night. One cannot be too careful when there are such characters lurking in the neighbourhood.'

The old lady went out to superintend the safe fastening of the house, without dreaming that he who caused her such alarm was dwelling under her own peaceful roof.

The next day nothing else was spoken of, and it was easy for me to draw from my uncle all that I wished to hear. I ascertained that the real cousin had not made a favourable impression; and that, in fact, they were all glad that the engagement between him and Jettè was at an end. My extraordinary and mysterious disappearance had set them all guessing, but they despaired of ever solving the riddle, since all the investigations and inquiries which could be quietly instituted had failed to yield the slightest trace of me. Gustav, following up the hint I had given in the note I had left, had written to a friend in Fredericia, but, of course, this had led to no result. Thomas daily scoured the country round, searching the woods and the moors to find me; but every succeeding day lessened his hopes of being able to bring me a prisoner to his home.

My imprudence, then, had been productive of no bad effects; fortune had befriended the rash fool, as it so often does. I cannot describe with what joy I gathered this happy intelligence; and when I had reflected on it for some days, I came to the conclusion that I *might* venture again to show myself at ---- Court, and entreat forgiveness of my sad delinquencies. I formed a thousand plans and relinquished them again. At length I wrote to Copenhagen for new clothes, and sent a letter, to be forwarded from thence by the post to the Justitsraad, wherein I made a confession, and candidly avowed all that my inclination for a frolic and a succession of accidental circumstances had led me into. I threw myself upon Miss Jettè's kindness to intercede for me, trusting that she would not refuse me this favour; I dwelt on my contrition and deep regret, and implored forgiveness for my misdemeanours. Nothing did I conceal, except my name and my love for Hannè. I hope, dear reader, that you will not find it necessary to ask why I concealed these.

The blue coat arrived at length from Copenhagen, with information that the letter had been forwarded. It was not difficult for me to put it into my uncle's head to drive over to ---- Court, and ascertain if there had been any elucidation of the mysterious story that had almost entirely chased sleep from my good aunt's couch. I had intended to have accompanied him, but when the time came my courage failed, and, pleading a headache, I left him to go alone.

'You are not well, my dear nephew, that I can easily perceive,' said he, as I saw him into his carriage; 'we must positively send for the doctor. You will turn quite black in the long run, for in a fortnight only you have become as dark as a Tartar, and that is not a healthy colour. Perhaps you have got worms.'

The worthy man little knew that I was purposely obliterating my good complexion more and more, and had the greatest trouble in giving myself this Tartar tint. 'He shall drink some of my decoction of wormwood,' said my aunt; 'it is better than any apothecary's mixtures, and will do him a great deal of good.' Whereupon she invited me to go with her to her sanctum, and there I was compelled to swallow a horrid bitter potion, which was enough to bring the most hardened sinner to a sense of his guilt.

'Well, tell me, have they found Morten Frederichsen?' asked my aunt, when my uncle returned. 'Has he broken in over yonder?'

'No, no, my dear. There was no housebreaker in question at all. Truly, it is a laughable story. The man has written the Justitsraad from Copenhagen.'

'Written? A threatening letter? A defiance? It is making nothing at all of the police--a positive insult to them. But, God be thanked, he is no longer in our neighbourhood.'

'Now, my good wife, you are quite mistaken,' replied my uncle, who then proceeded to relate the contents of my letter, which, it appeared, had still further excited the baffled curiosity of the worthy family.

My aunt could not recover from the state of amazement into which she had been thrown.

'But what says the Justitsraad?' I asked.

'Why, what can he say? He is glad that the intruder was a gentleman, for the letter is evidently written by one in that rank of life, but of course he is angry at having been so hoaxed. But it was Jettè who pacified him, for she did not stop entreating him until he promised her not to vex himself any longer about the matter. I thought of you, nephew, and took the opportunity to say a few words about forgiveness and placability, grounding my lesson of Christian duty on the excellent admonitions of the Scriptures. They talked a great deal about the mysterious personage; and the Justitsraad said at length that he would not wreak his vengeance upon him if he could see him, but would rather feel a pleasure in meeting him again. The girls wanted their father to put an advertisement in the papers addressed in a roundabout way to him, but Mr. Holm dissuaded them from this.'

'That was very right of Mr. Holm,' said my aunt. 'He is a sensible young man; for if the person really was a thief--of which there can be no doubt--for he who tells a lie will also steal ...'

'That does not by any means follow, dear aunt,' said I.

'Well, be that as it may, we are invited to ---- Court to-morrow, and I promised that we would go, and you, too, Adolph. I told them I had a nephew on a visit to me at present.'

'I ... but ... you know, uncle, my father and the Justitsraad ...'

'Oh, we must manage to set all that to-rights; to entertain feelings of enmity is quite unworthy of two such men. Leave the matter to me. I have not yet mentioned your name, therefore you need be under no embarrassment in presenting yourself to the Justitsraad. He is a very pleasant man.'

'Sooner or later--it makes but little difference,' thought I; 'and if I can but look him full in the face, without dreading to be discovered, I shall be willing to acknowledge all his good qualities.'

'Had we not better take the bottle of wormwood with us in the carriage?' said my aunt, next day. 'Adolph looks so black under the eyes this morning, that I am sure he is worse than he was yesterday.'

'I confess I do not like his looks,' said my uncle; 'but perhaps that dark shade is cast by his moustaches. One might really fancy, nephew, that you had darkened your face with burnt cork. You don't look at all like yourself. Truly, the rifle corps has a great deal to answer for.'

My endeavours had been successful. Instead of the gay, fresh-looking, light-hearted cousin, in a dark-green frock-coat, that had left ---- Court, came, along with the clergyman and his lady, a grave, silent, dark-haired nephew, in a blue coat; with an olive complexion, very sallow, and with black moustaches; my transformation was complete. I scarcely recognized myself when I saw myself in the glass. The worst that could happen would be to be taken for myself--the agreeably characterized *'sad scamp'* from Hamburg. But for what would I not be taken to see Hannè again!

None of them knew me; the Justitsraad addressed me as 'Mr. Adolph,' and received me very courteously. The guests were Kammerraad Tvede, the Jutlander, and his family, Gustav, a friend of his, and ourselves. I do not doubt that my heightened colour might have been visible even through the swarthy shade of my cheek when Hannè entered the room. She had become ten times prettier than ever in these fourteen days; she looked really quite captivating. Gustav and Jettè cast many speaking glances at each other, and her mother looked kindly at them. I stood silent and grave in a corner window; the various feelings that rushed upon me assisted me in playing the part of a somewhat embarrassed stranger. Watchel rose from his mat, and walked round the room as if to greet his master's well-known guests; he wagged his tail in token of welcome to my uncle and aunt, but he growled at me, whereupon Hannè called him away, and made him lie down in his usual place.

'But tell me, my dear friend, how does this happen? When I was here last your daughter was engaged to another gentleman. What has become of him?' said the inquisitive neighbour, Tvede.

'Oh, that was only a jest from their childhood,' said the Justitsraad. 'He was my brother's son, and was on a visit to us. Jettè was betrothed at that time to Mr. Holm, though her engagement was not generally known.'

'Oh, indeed; but where is your nephew now?'

'He left us some time ago.'

'A very nice young man your nephew is; perhaps what was only jest between him and the elder sister may become earnest between him and the younger one. What say you to that, Miss Hannè?'

Hannè blushed scarlet, but made no answer. The Justitsraad looked a little confused, and smiled to my uncle; I sat as if on thorns.

'So your father resides in Copenhagen, Mr. Adolph?' said the indefatigable questioner, turning towards me.

I rose in a fright, and bowed.

'He is a merchant, is he not? and has a good deal to do with the West Indies?'

'Yes, he has a good deal to do with the West Indies,' I replied, in a feigned voice, as different from my own as I possibly could make it.

'My brother-in-law does a great deal of business with the provinces also--commission-business--as a corn-merchant,' said my uncle; 'that is safer than West India business.'

'Ah, so he is your brother-in-law--married to your sister, no doubt? Well, your nephew seems a fine young man. He is in the army, I suppose?'

'No, my dear sir, he is a clerk in his father's office; but as he has joined a rifle corps, according to a new regulation he is obliged to have moustaches,' replied my uncle, honestly believing the truth of my assertion.

The observation of all present was drawn upon me. I turned crimson. Gustav and his friend cast a meaning glance at each other, and both smiled, I interpreted the smile into this, 'He is a vain, conceited puppy; the regulation is the coinage of his own brain.' What an unmerciful interpreter is conscience! We were to take our coffee in the garden; thither, therefore, we all proceeded. I approached Jettè, and began to talk to her about the pretty country round.

'Have you been long at your uncle's?' she asked.

'I have been there some little time, and I should have left it before now, had not a strange commission been imposed on me--one which I find it very difficult to fulfil. It is a commission which relates to the family here,' I added, when I found she was not inclined to ask any questions.

'To us?' said Jettè; 'and the commission is so difficult?'

'It is no other than to obtain for a man the restoration of that peace of mind of which his inconsiderate folly has deprived him, and to procure for him your father's forgiveness--his pardon of an injury that otherwise will weigh him down with regret and remorse for the remainder of his life.'

Jettè looked at me in astonishment.

'What--Mr. Adolph? I do not understand.'

'A friend of mine has written to me from Copenhagen, and charged me to try and make his peace with the Justitsraad; but the papers which he has forwarded to me containing his case, really present it in such a perplexing and unfortunate light, that I cannot attempt to carry out his wishes, unless you, to whom he particularly desired me first to apply, will grant me your valuable assistance. He certainly did most shamefully abuse your confidence.'

'You know ... it is ... you are acquainted with that strange story?' exclaimed Jettè, much embarrassed.

'I know it thoroughly; and though this is the first time I have had the honour of seeing you, I think I may say you yourself are not better acquainted with the particulars of that affair than I am. It is on your kindness that I principally rely; yet I may not mention my friend's name until he has obtained entire forgiveness. He has given me very positive directions.'

'I cannot but be much surprised that a person who insulted my father and us all so much, should ...'

'Insulted you, my dear young lady? I am shocked to hear it; I am sorry that he should have written me what was not true; his letter led me to believe that, on the contrary, he had rather been of service to you.'

Jettè blushed deeply, and I thought I perceived tears in her eyes. 'He shall certainly not find me ungrateful,' she said; 'I have not forgotten what I owe him. What do you require of me?'

'My friend entreats you, through me, to grant him your forgiveness for a mystification to which purely accidental circumstances led at first, but which was continued solely from an interest in your fate, and an anxious desire to serve you. He entreats that you will use your influence to mollify your father towards him, and procure for me a private interview with him, which I trust will end in the pardon of my friend, who has no dearer wish than to be received again into a circle he so highly esteems and respects, and to be permitted to prove to them how deeply he regrets his thoughtless folly.'

Some others of the same party now approached, and I was obliged to drop the conversation. Gustave and Hannè were disputing.

'Jeer at me as you will,' said Hannè, 'I hold to my opinion, that nothing is so tiresome as family connections. If one only could choose one's kindred those sort of ties would be much stronger. It is a pity not to go a step further, and let it be a fixed rule, that relations to a certain extent remote, should marry whether they suit each other or not. This would certainly extirpate *love*, but it would be vastly convenient, and in a recent case it would have hindered many doubts and hopes, and all that followed.'

'Pray recollect your last election; there was not much to boast of in him. The ties of consanguinity could hardly have furnished any family with a less desirable member.'

'Yes they could, for the member who came after him was much inferior, notwithstanding he bore on his brow the stamp of legitimacy. Even though my "election," as you call it, fell upon one who was treacherous, he was at any rate pleasant, lively, and amusing, whereas the legitimate one was cold, stupid, pedantic, tiresome; wearying one with every slow word he uttered. You do not mean one syllable of all the evil you speak of the stranger. The properly installed cousins and nephews whom I have latterly seen have been miserable creatures, who looked as if they could not count five, and as if they had not a thought to bestow on anything but their own pitiful persons, on which they placed the most exorbitant value, without the slightest grounds for so doing.'

As she finished this tirade, Hannè cast a side-glance at me, who, in truth, played capitally the part of the most tiresome, self-satisfied blockhead of a nephew anyone could imagine. She had no conception how part of her harangue had enchanted me.

'Legitimate right is a good thing; in that I quite agree with the young lady,' said the Jutlander, who had just approached us, and thought fit to join in the conversation. He had only caught a word or two of what Hannè had been saying, and mistook entirely her meaning.

While we continued to stroll about, Jettè took her sister aside, and whispered something to her. Hannè turned her eyes full on me, and looked keenly at me. As soon as it was possible, I went up to her, and began to talk about the weather, that invariable preface to even the most important and most interesting subjects. We soon fell into conversation, and it turned upon the communication Jettè had just made.

'My sister tells me that your friend is anxious to obtain our forgiveness,' said she. 'We have already given him that, for he has done us a greater service than he thinks. Our regard is another affair; that would be more difficult to bestow, and doubtless he does not entertain the slightest idea of ever winning it.'

'You would condemn him to a severe doom if you would forbid his striving at least to deserve it. Without your good opinion, your forgiveness would be a mere passing act of charity; without the former he would be a beggar all his life, with it *he would become a millionnaire*.'

Hannè coloured at the reminiscences these words awakened; but she only said,

'You put a high value on it.'

'Not higher than my friend does. *Your* regard, charming Miss Hannè, is what he seeks, and were he not attracted to this place by a perhaps too vivid *souvenir* of you, I should not be standing here as his spokesman. Your sister has kindly promised to obtain for me a few minutes' private conversation with your father; if your hatred of my unfortunate friend cannot be softened, tell me so, I pray you, at once, and I shall spare your father a communication which may perhaps remind him of disagreeable impressions, for without your entire pardon I cannot fulfil my errand, and I will not attempt to do it by halves.'

'You are a very zealous agent, there is no denying that. Well, you may speak to my father; I will not be the most hard-hearted of the family. Besides, I really feel that your friend has an advocate in my own inclination for a joke, though his jest was carried rather too far.'

'I expected this goodness from you, or my friend would not have painted you in true colours.'

'And pray in what colours did he paint me, if I may venture to ask? It would be difficult to give anyone's likeness on so short an acquaintance.'

'They were as radiant as if he had borrowed for his pencil tints from heaven to do justice to the original ... He adores you, to say the absolute truth.'

'Indeed! He really does me too much honour,' she said, stiffly, and in an offended tone of voice.

At the 'tints from heaven,' and 'justice to the original,' she had smiled; at the 'absolute truth,' she became angry.

We were at the foot of the hillock, on which stood the swing.

'There must be a fine view from the top of that rising ground,' said I.

Politeness obliged her to ascend the bank. Gustav and his friend followed us at a little distance in earnest conversation; the rest of the party had gone to the summer-house, where coffee was prepared.

'Really, this is a lovely view!' I remarked, mechanically.

'Yonder lies your uncle's church,' said Hannè; 'it makes the twelfth spire we can see from this hill.'

'I have remarked this place from my uncle's window; these white poles shine out against the dark-green background.'

'Were you afraid of them? Did you fancy they were ...'

'A gallows!' I exclaimed, interrupting her. 'No, Miss Hannè; I am rather more rational than my foolish friend.'

Hannè looked inquisitively at me.

'Have you remembered what he begged of you on this spot? That when you heard evil of him, and doubts of his honour, you would come up here, and judge leniently of the absent; that you would not condemn him totally, although appearances might be against him?'

'He must have favoured you with a remarkably minute report of his sayings and doings here,' said Hannè, laughing. 'You have got his speeches by heart--word for word.'

'Every word which he exchanged with you remains for ever engraved on his memory. You promised this to him. Dare he flatter himself that you have not forgotten that promise, and have not deserted him, while he relied on your compassion?'

'I have taken his part a great deal more than he deserves,' she replied. 'But now that is no longer necessary, and if he return here, he shall find me his worst enemy, for I do not allow myself to be made a fool of without taking my revenge.'

'Have some mercy, fair lady! See, I sue for grace--he cannot stand your ire. I have come to throw myself at your feet--acquitted by you, he will have courage to meet any storm ... Miss Hannè,' I added, with my own natural voice, 'you are the only one who knows that the unfortunate sinner is here; condemn me irrevocably, if you have the heart to do so--I will hear my sentence from your lips.'

Hannè looked at me with an arch smile.

'You will not betray me, or misuse my confidence,' I added, in a supplicatory tone. 'Bestow on me your forgiveness, and procure for me that of your parents. Without this I cannot live. You have discovered me, notwithstanding my disguise; it was only under its shelter that I ventured to come near you during the light of day. Ah! at night, I have often been here, standing outside of the house, looking up at your window, until the light was extinguished in your room, and I had no longer any evidence of your proximity to feast upon.'

She looked at me for a moment with unusual softness,--nay, with kindness; then clapping her hands together, she called out,

'Gustav! Linden! Come here--make haste! Here he is--here he is!'

'Who? What is it?' cried the two young men, as they came hurrying towards us.

'For Heaven's sake--Miss Hannè--you surely will not ... you abuse the confidence I placed in you--I did not expect this of you. Will you betray me? Will you disgrace me before that stranger?' I stammered out, amazed and vexed at her sudden change.

'There he is--the false cousin--standing yonder. Now he is caught,' added Hannè, skipping about with joy.

'The cousin--he!' exclaimed Gustav, in great astonishment; 'but tell me then ...'

'Mr. Holm,' said I, 'and you, sir, with whom I have not the pleasure of being acquainted ...'

'True!' cried Hannè, interrupting me, 'I owe you an explanation. You need not excuse yourself to Gustav, in his heart he acknowledges you to be his benefactor; and this gentleman, *with whom you have not the pleasure of being acquainted,* is quite as cognisant of your exploits as any of us. "You will not betray me, or misuse my confidence,"' said she, mimicking me, 'therefore let me present to you Mr. Linden, my bridegroom elect. You once asked me what this ring I wear betokened--do you remember that? I was then obliged to give you an evasive answer; now I will confide the secret to you, my much honoured cousin--and much admired truth-teller.'

Could I have guessed *this,* or have had the slightest suspicion of it, two hours earlier, I never again would have put my feet within the doors of ---- Court.

There was nothing for it now but to let myself patiently be dragged about by them, after I had muttered something, that might as well have been taken for a malediction as a felicitation.

My uncle was walking in the alley of pine-trees with the Justitsraad and Jettè; she had been preparing him for the audience I told her I wished of him, but she had not yet the least idea that I was the person for whom she had been pleading. I appeared before them as a poor culprit.

'Dear father,' said Hannè, 'I bring a deserter, who has given himself up to me. He relies on your forgiveness, for which I have become surety, and if you withhold it, my word will be broken.'

'Let me speak, child,' said my uncle, who fancied that a disagreement between my father and the Justitsraad was the affair in question.

'As the servant of the Lord, it is my duty to exhort everyone to peace, and forgiveness of injuries; you should all remember the divine mission of Him who is the fountain of love, and who came to bring goodwill on earth; remembering His example you should chase away hatred, and all evil passions and thoughts from your mind. See, this young person comes to you with confiding hope, and now do shake hands with him in sign of reconciliation, and let not two worthy men remain longer enemies. Speak kindly to him, my old friend, and do not oblige him longer to conceal his name, because it is one which you once disliked--let the past be now forgotten!'

'What, *you* also pleading for him, my worthy friend? Then, indeed, I must give in. Well, the foolish madcap has found intercessors enough, I think,' said the Justitsraad, as he held out his hand to me.

'He is petitioning for his friend,' said Jettè.

'For my benefactor,' said Gustav.

'For his old father,' said my uncle.

'For himself,' said Hannè. 'This is the pretended cousin himself, in disguise; this is the very man himself who threw our family into such confusion; but what his real name may be, Heaven only knows.'

'He is my sister's son--Adolph Kerner, a son of Mr. Kerner, the well-known Copenhagen merchant; he has no need to be ashamed of his name,' said my uncle.

Everyone was astonished; there was a general silence from amazement.

At length Jettè exclaimed, 'The pretended cousin himself?'

'The young Kerner who went to Hamburg?' asked the Justitsraad.

'What! the impostor my own nephew?' cried my uncle, upon whom the truth began to dawn. The formidable explanation was given, forgiveness followed, and we were reconciled. The Justitsraad shook hands with me cordially.

'And now let us seek my mother,' said Hannè, 'and fall at her feet. For the honour of our sex, I hope Mr. Kerner will have to undergo the pains of purgatory in her presence.'

We proceeded to the summer-house where the rest of the party were sitting at table, taking coffee. The Justitsraad led me up to his wife, and said, 'I beg to present to you your lost nephew, who returns, like the prodigal son, and begs for forgiveness. Tomorrow he will show himself without these moustaches, in his own fair hair, and he hopes to find the same kind aunt in you whom the false cousin Carl learned so speedily to love.'

The lady gave me her hand, after having held up her finger as if to threaten me.

'And here you see Morten Frederichsen, my dear, against whom Sultan was to have guarded our house. The good-for-nothing, he has certainly hoaxed all us old ones,' said my uncle, laughing. 'His liver-complaint was nothing but a trick.'

'What is that you say? Morten Frederichsen! How the idea of that dreadful creature frightened me! But I have retaliated upon him with my wormwood, I rather think.' The good woman was much puzzled, and could hardly comprehend how it all came about.

'And now I beg to introduce to Kammerraad Tvede, the younger Kerner, son of Mr. Kerner of Copenhagen, a youth who has lately returned from an educational trip to Hamburg,' said the mischief-loving Hannè, pulling me up to the Jutlander.

'A very fine young man,' stammered the Kammerraad. 'I have the pleasure of knowing your father, and am aware of the high standing of your house.'

I made my escape over to Jettè and Gustav, who kindly took compassion on me.

'Don't you all see now that it was not so stupid of me to propose examining him in the almanack?' said Hannè.

'At any rate, to *you* belongs the credit of having placed me in the most painful dilemma,' said I, with some bitterness. 'Be merciful now, and do not play with me as a cat does with a mouse; the conqueror can afford to be magnanimous to the vanquished.'

'Well, the sun is about to set, and I suppose I must let my just resentment go with it. I will forgive you for all your misdemeanours upon one condition, that, according to our late agreement, you will return by-and-by, and assist us in getting up some private theatricals, to which I have the pleasure of inviting all now present. I think you will shine in "*The April Fools*."'[6]

'Shame on you all!' cried Jettè. 'How can you be so revengeful, and still persecute Mr. Kerner in this inhuman way?'

'I trust he will excuse the persecution,' said her father; 'and I hope that it will not frighten him from a house which will always be open to him, and where he will henceforth be as well received under his own name as he was under that of--Cousin Carl.'

THE DOOMED HOUSE BY B. S. INGEMANN

'The house near Christianshavn's canal is again for sale--your worthy uncle's house, Johanna! and now upon very reasonable terms,' said the young joiner and cabinet-maker, Frants, one morning to his pretty wife, as he laid the advertisement sheet of the newspaper upon the cradle, and glanced at his little boy, an infant of about three months old, who was sleeping sweetly, and seemed to be sporting with heavenly cherubs in his innocent dreams.

'Let us on no account think of the dear old house,' replied his wife, taking up the newspaper and placing it on the table, without even looking at the advertisement. 'We have a roof over our heads as long as Mr. Stork will have patience about the rent. If we have bread enough for ourselves, and for yon little angel, who will soon begin to want some, we may well rest contented. Notwithstanding our poverty, we are, perhaps, the happiest married couple in the whole town,' she added gently, and with an affectionate smile, 'and we ought to thank our God that he did not let the wide world separate us from each other, but permitted you to return from your distant journey, healthy and cheerful, and that he has granted us love and strength to bear our little cross with patience.'

'You are ever the same amiable and pious Johanna,' said Frants, embracing the lovely young mother, who reminded him of an exquisite picture of the Madonna he had seen abroad, 'and you have made me better and more patient than I was, either by nature or by habit. But I really cannot remain longer in this miserable garret--I have neither room nor spirits to work here; and if I am to make anything by my handicraft, I must have a proper workshop, and space to breathe in and to move in.

'Your good uncle's house, near the canal, is just the place for me; how many jovial songs my old master and I have sung there together over our joiner's bench! Ah! *then* I shall feel comfortable and at home. It was there, also, that I first saw you--there, that I used to sit every evening with you in the nice little parlour, with the cheerful green wainscoting, when I came from the workshop with old Mr. Flok. I remember how, on Sundays and on holidays, he used to take his silver goblet from the cupboard in the alcove, and drink with me in such a sociable way. And when my piece of trial-work as a journeyman was finished, and the large, handsome coffin was put out in state in the workshop, do you remember how glad the old man was, and how you sank into my arms when he placed your hand in mine, over the coffin, and said:

'"Take her, Frants, and be worthy of her! My house shall be your home and hers, and everything it contains shall be your property when I am sleeping in this coffin, awaiting a blessed resurrection."'

'Ah! but all that never came to pass,' sighed Johanna; 'the coffin lies empty up in yonder loft, and frightens children in the dark. The dear old house is under the ban of evil report, and no one will buy it, or even hire it, now, so many strange, unfortunate deaths have taken place there.'

'These very circumstances are in our favour, Johanna; on account of this state of things Mr. Stork will sell it at a great bargain, and give a half year's credit for the purchase-money. In the course of six months, surely, the long-protracted settlement of your uncle's affairs will be brought to a close, and we shall, at least, have as much as will pay what we owe. The house will then be our own, and you will see how happy and prosperous we shall be. Surely, it is not the fault of the poor house that three children died there of measles, and two people of old age, in the course of a few months; and none but silly old women can be frightened because the idle children in the street choose to scratch upon the walls, "*The Doomed House*." The house is, and always will be, liked by me, and if Mr. Stork will accept of my offer for it, without any other security than my own word, that dwelling shall be mine to-day, and we can move into it to-morrow.'

'Oh, my dear Frants, you cannot think how reluctant I am to increase our debt to this Mr. Stork. Believe me, he is not a good man, however friendly and courteous he may seem to be. Even my uncle could not always tolerate him, though it was not in his nature to dislike any of God's creatures. Whenever Mr. Stork came, and began to talk about business and bills--my uncle became silent and gloomy, and always gave me a wink to retire to my chamber.'

'I know very well Mr. Stork was looking after you then,' said Frants, with a smile of self-satisfaction, 'but *I* was a more fortunate suitor. It was a piece of folly on the part of the old bachelor; all that, however, is forgotten now, and he has transferred the regard he once had for you to me. He never duns me for my rent, he lent me money at the time of the child's baptism, and he shows me more kindness than anyone else does.'

'But I cannot endure the way in which he looks at me, Frants, and I put no faith either in his friendship or his rectitude. The very house that he is now about to sell he hardly came honestly by, as he gives out--and I cannot understand how he has so large a claim upon the property my uncle left; I never heard my uncle speak of it. God only knows what will remain for us when all these heavy claims that have been brought forward are satisfied; yet my uncle was considered a rich man.'

'The lawyers and the proper court must settle that,' replied Frants; 'I only know this, that I should be a fool if I did not buy the house now.'

'But to say the truth, dear Frants,' urged Johanna, in a supplicating tone, 'I am almost afraid to go back to that house, dear as every corner of it has been to me from my childhood. I cannot reconcile myself to the reality of the painful circumstances said to have attended my poor uncle's death. And whenever I pass over *Long Bridge*, and near the Dead-house for the drowned, with its low windows, I always feel an irresistible impulse to look in, and see if he is not there still, waiting to be placed in his proper coffin, and decently buried in a churchyard.'

'Ah--your brain is conjuring up a parcel of old nursery tales, my Johanna! We have nothing to fear from your good, kind uncle. If indeed his spirit could be near us, here on earth, it would only bring us blessings and happiness. I am quite easy on that score; he was a pious, God-fearing man, and there was nothing in his life to disturb his repose after death. Report said that he had drowned himself on purpose, but I am quite convinced that was not true. If I had not unluckily been away on my travels as a journeyman, and you with your dying aunt--your mother's sister, we would most likely have had him with us now. How often I have warned him against sailing about alone in Kalleboe Bay! But he would go every Sunday. As long as I was in his employ, I always made a point of accompanying him, and when I went away he promised me never to go without a boatman.'

'Alas! that was an unfortunate Christmas!' sighed Johanna, 'it was not until he had been advertised as missing in the newspapers, and Mr. Stork had recognized his corpse at the Dead-house for the drowned, and had caused him to be secretly buried as a suicide,--it was not until all this was over, that I knew he had not been put into his own coffin, and laid in consecrated ground.'

'Let us not grieve longer, dear Johanna, for what it was not in our power to prevent; but let us rather, in respect to the memory of our kind benefactor, put the house in order which he occupied and where he worked for us, inhabit it cheerfully, and rescue it from mysterious accusations and evil reports. *Our* welfare was all he thought of, and laboured for.'

'As you will then, dear Frants!' said Johanna, yielding to his arguments. She hastened at the same moment to take up from its cradle the child, who had just awoke, and holding it out to its young father, she added, 'May God protect this innocent infant, and spare it to us!'

Frants kissed the mother and the child, smoothed his brown hair, and taking his hat down from its peg, he hurried off to conclude the purchase on which he had set his heart.

He returned in great spirits, and the next day the little family removed to the house which belonged to Mr. Flok, Frants was rejoiced to see his old master's furniture, which he had bought at an auction, restored to its former place, and he felt almost as if the easy-chair and the bureau, formerly in the immediate use of the old man, must share in his gladness. But the baker's wife at the corner of the street shrugged her shoulders, and pitied the handsome young couple, whom she considered doomed to sickness and misfortune, because five corpses within the last six months had been carried out of that house; and because there was an inscription on its walls, that however often it had been effaced had always reappeared. 'Et Forbandet Haus'--'The Doomed House'--stood there, written in red characters, and all the old crones in the neighbourhood affirmed that the words were *written in blood!*

'Mark my words,' said the baker's wife at the corner of the street, to her daughter, 'before the year is at an end, we shall have another coffin carried out of that house.'

Frants the joiner had bestirred himself to set all to rights in the long-neglected workshop, and Johanna had put the house in nice order, and arranged everything as it used to be in days gone by. The little parlour, with the green wainscoting and the old fashioned alcove, had its former chairs and tables replaced in it; the bureau occupied its ancient corner, and the easy-chair again stood near the stove, and seemed to await its master's return. Often, as the young couple sat together in the twilight, while the blaze of the fire in the stove cast a cheerful glare through its little grated door on the hearth beneath, they missed the old man, and talked of him with sadness and affection. But Johanna would sometimes glance timidly at the empty leather arm-chair--and when the moon shone in through the small window panes, she would at times even fancy that she saw her uncle sitting there--but pale and bloody, and with dripping wet hair.

She would then exclaim, 'Let us have lights; the baby seems restless. I must see what is the matter with it.'

One evening there were no candles downstairs. She had to go for them up to the storeroom in the garret. She lighted a small taper that was in the lantern, and went out of the room, while Frants rocked the infant's cradle to lull it to sleep. But she had only been a few minutes gone, when he heard a noise as if of some one having fallen down in the loft above, and he also thought he heard Johanna scream; he quitted the cradle instantly, and rushing upstairs after her, he found her lying in a swoon near the coffin, with the lantern in her hand, though its light was extinguished. Exceedingly alarmed he carried her downstairs, relighted the taper, and used every effort to recover her from her fainting fit. When she was better, and somewhat composed, he asked in much anxiety what had happened. 'Oh! I am as timid as a foolish child,' said Johanna. 'It was only my poor uncle's coffin up yonder that frightened me. I would have begged you to go and fetch the candles, but I was ashamed to own my silly fears, and when the current of air blew out the light in my lantern up there, it seemed to me as if a spectre's death-cold breathing passed over my face, and I fancied I saw amidst the gloom the lid of the coffin rising--so I fainted away in my childish terror.'

'That coffin shall not frighten you again,' said Frants, 'I will advertise it to-morrow for sale.' He did so, but ineffectually, for no one bought it.

One day Mr. Stork made his appearance, bringing with him the contract and deed of sale.

He was a tall, strongly-built man, with a countenance by no means pleasant, though it almost always wore a smile; but the smile, if narrowly scrutinized, had a sinister expression, and seemed to convulse his features. He sported a gaudy waistcoat, and was dressed like an old bachelor, who was going on some matrimonial expedition, and wished to conceal his age. This day he was even more complaisant than usual, praised the beauty of the infant, remarked its likeness to its lovely mother, and offered Frants a loan of money to purchase new furniture, and make any improvements he might wish in the interior of the house. Franks thanked him, but declined the offer, assuring him that he was quite satisfied with the house and furniture as they were, and wished everything about him to wear its former aspect. However, he said, he certainly would like to enlarge the workshop by adding to it the old lumber-room at the back of the house, the entrance to which he found was closed.

Mr. Stork then informed him that there was a door on the opposite side of the lumber-room, which opened into the house *he* occupied, and that he had lately been using this empty place as a cellar for his firewood; but he readily promised to have it cleared out as speedily as possible, and to have the entrance into his own house stopped up.

'Yet,' he added, in a very gracious manner, 'it is hardly necessary to have any separation between the two houses, when I have such respectable and agreeable neighbours as yourselves.'

'What made you look so crossly at that excellent Mr. Stork, Johanna?' asked her husband, when their visitor was gone. 'I am sure he is kindness itself. He cannot really help that he has that unfortunate contortion of the mouth, which gives a peculiar expression to his countenance.'

'I sincerely wish we had some other person as our neighbour, and had nothing to do with him!' exclaimed Johanna. 'I do not feel safe with such a man near us.'

Frants now worked with equal diligence and patience--and often remained until a late hour in the workshop, especially if he had any order to finish. He preferred cabinet-making to the more common branches of his trade, and was always delighted when he had any pretty piece of furniture to construct from one of the finer sorts of wood. But he was best known as a coffin-maker, and necessity compelled him to undertake more of this gloomy kind of work than he liked. Often when he was finishing a coffin, he would reflect upon all the sorrow, and perhaps calamity which the work, that provided him and his with bread, would bring into the house into which it was destined to enter. And when he met people in high health and spirits, on the public promenades, he frequently sighed to think how soon he might be engaged in nailing together the last earthly resting-places of these animated forms.

One night he was so much occupied in finishing a large coffin, that he did not remark how late it had become, until he heard the watchman call out 'Twelve.'

At that moment he fancied he heard a hollow voice behind him say,

'Still hammering! And for whom is that coffin?'

He started--dropped the hammer from his hand--and looked round in terror, but no one was to be seen.

'It is the old gloomy thoughts creeping back into my mind, and affecting my brain, now at this ghastly hour of midnight,' said he; but he put away the hammer and nails, and took up his light to go to his bed-room. Before he reached the door of the workshop, however, the candle which had burned down very low--quite in the socket of the candlestick, suddenly went out. He was left in the dark, and in vain he groped about to find the door--at any other time he would have laughed at the circumstance, but now it rather added to his annoyance that three times he found himself at the door of the lumber-room, instead of getting hold of the one which opened into his house. The third time he came to it, he stopped and listened, for he fancied he heard something moving within the empty room; a light also glimmered through a chink in the door which was fastened, and on listening more attentively he thought he distinctly heard a sound as if buckets of water were being dashed over the floor, and some one scrubbing it with a brush. 'It is an odd time to scour the floor,' he thought, and then knocking at the door, and raising his voice--he called out loudly to ask who was there, and what they were doing at so late an hour. At that moment the light disappeared, and all became as still as death.

'I must have been mistaken,' thought Frants, as he again tried to find the door he had at first sought. In spite of himself, a dread of some evil--or of something supernatural, seemed to haunt him, and the image of his old master--who was drowned--appeared before him in that dark workshop, where they had spent so many cheerful hours together. At last he found the door, and retired as quickly as possible to his chamber, where his wife and child were both fast asleep. He, too, at length fell asleep, but he was restless in his slumbers, and disturbed by strange dreams. In the course of the night he dreamed that his wife's uncle, Mr. Flok, stood before him, and said,

'Why was I not placed in my coffin? Why was I not laid in a Christian burying-ground? Seek, and you will find--destroy the curse, before it destroys you also!'

In the morning when he awoke he looked so pale and ill that Johanna was quite alarmed; but he did not like to frighten her by telling her his dreams, and, indeed, he was ashamed at the impression they had made upon himself, for, notwithstanding all the confidence he had expressed on coming to the house, he could not help feeling nervous and uncomfortable.

Nor did the unpleasant sensation wear off, his gay spirits vanished, and he was also unhappy because the time was approaching when the purchase-money for the house would become due, and the settlement of the old man's affairs, to which he had looked forward in expectation of obtaining his wife's inheritance, seemed to be as far off as ever. He found it difficult to meet the small daily expenses of his family, and he feared the threatening future.

'Seek and you will find!' he repeated to himself; 'destroy the curse before it destroys you! What curse? I begin to fear that there really is some evil doom connected with this house.'

It was also a very unaccountable circumstance that however often he scratched out the mysterious inscription from the wall--'The Doomed House'--it appeared again next day in characters as fresh and red as ever. His health began to give way under all his anxiety, and the child also became ill. One evening he had been taking a solitary walk to a spot which had now a kind of morbid fascination for him--the Dead-house for the drowned--and when he returned home, he found Johanna weeping by the cradle of her suffering infant.

'You were right,' he exclaimed, 'we were happier in our humble garret than in this ill-fated house. Would that we had remained there! Tell me, Johanna, of what are you thinking? Has the doctor been here? What does he say of our dear little one?'

'If it should get worse towards night, there lies our last hope,' she replied, pointing towards the table.

Frants took up the prescription, and gazed on the incomprehensible Latin words, as if therein he would have read his fate. The tears stood in his eyes.

'And to-morrow,' said Johanna, 'to-morrow will be a day of misery. Have you any means of paying Mr. Stork?'

'None whatever! But *that* is a small evil compared to *this*,' he answered, as he pointed to the feverish and moaning infant. 'Have you been to the workshop?' he continued, after a pause, 'the large coffin is finished; perhaps it may be our own last home--it would hold us all!'

'Oh! if that could only be!' exclaimed Johanna, as she threw her arms round him. 'Could we only all three be removed together to a better world, there would be no more sorrow for us! But the hour of separation is close at hand; to-morrow, if you cannot pay Mr. Stork, you will be cast into prison, and I shall sit alone here with that dying child!'

'What do you say? Cast into prison! How do you know that? Has that man been here frightening you? He has not hinted a syllable of such a threat to me.'

Johanna then related to him how Mr. Stork had latterly often called, under pretence of wishing to see Frants, but always when he was out. He had made himself very much at home, and had overwhelmed her with compliments and flattering speeches; he had also declared frequently that he would not trouble Frants for the money he owed him, if she would pay the debt in another manner. At first, she said, she did not understand him, and when she *did* comprehend his meaning, she did not like to mention it to Frants, for fear of his taking the matter up warmly, and quarrelling with Stork, which would bring ruin on himself. Mr. Stork, however, had become more bold and presuming, and that very evening, on her repelling his advances and desiring him to quit her presence, he had threatened that if she mentioned a syllable of what had passed to her husband, nay, farther, if she were not prepared to change her behaviour towards himself before another sun had set, Frants should be thrown into prison for debt, and might congratulate himself in that pleasant abode on the fidelity of his wife.

'Well,' said Frants, with forced composure, 'he has got me in his toils--but his pitiful baseness shall not crush me. I have, indeed, been blind not to detect the villany that lay behind that satanic smile, and improvident to let myself be deluded by his pretended friendship. But if the Almighty will only spare and protect you, and that dear child, I shall not lose courage. Be comforted, my Johanna!'

It was now growing late--the child awoke from the restless sleep of fever--it seemed worse, and Frants ran to an apothecary with the prescription. 'The last hope!' he sighed, as he hurried along; 'and if it should fail--who will console poor Johanna to-morrow evening, when I am in a prison, and she has to clad the child in its grave clothes! Oh, how we shall miss you--sweet little angel! Was *this* the happiness I dreamt of in the old house? Yes--people are right--it *is* accursed!'

The apothecary's shop was closed, but the prescription had been taken in through a little aperture in the door, and Frants sat down on the stone steps to wait until the medicine was ready. It was a clear, starry December night, but the sorrowing father sat shivering in the cold, and gazing gloomily on the frozen pavement--he was not thinking of the stars or of the skies. The watchman passed and bade him 'good morning.'

'It will be a good morning, indeed, for me,' thought poor Frants. 'A morning fraught with despair.'

At that moment the clock of a neighbouring church struck *one*, and the watchman sang, in a full, bass voice, these simple words:

'Help us, O Jesus dear!
Our earthly cross to bear;
Oh! grant us patience *here*,
And be our Saviour *there!*'

Frants heard the pious song, and a change seemed to come over his spirit--he raised his saddened eye to the magnificent heavens above--gazed at the calm stars which studded the deep blue vault--clasped his hands and joined in the watchman's concluding words--

'Redeemer, grant Thy blessed help
To make our burden light.'

A small phial with the medicine was just then handed out to him, through the little sliding window; he paid his last coin for it, and, full of hope that *his* burden might be lightened, hastened to his home.

'Did you hear what the watchman was singing, Johanna?' asked Frants, when he entered the little green parlour, where the young mother was watching by her child.

'Hush, hush,' she whispered, 'he has fallen into an easy and quiet sleep. God will have pity upon us--our child will do well now.'

'Why, Johanna, you look as happy as if an angel from heaven had been with you, telling you blessed truths.'

'Yes, blessed truths have, as it were, been communicated to me from heaven!' replied Johanna, pointing to an old Bible which lay open upon the table. 'Look! this is my good uncle's family Bible--that I have not seen since he died, and God forgive me--I have thought too little lately of my Bible. I found this one to-night far back on the highest shelf of the alcove--and its holy words have given me strength and comfort. Read this passage, Frants, about putting our whole trust in the Lord, whatever may befall us.'

Frants read the portion pointed out to him, and then began to turn over the leaves of the well-worn, silver-clasped book. He found a number of pieces of paper here and there, but as he saw at a glance that they were only accounts and receipts, he did not care to examine them, but his attention was suddenly caught by a paper which appeared to be part of a journal kept by the old man, the last year of his life. He looked through it eagerly, Johanna observed with surprise how his countenance was darkening. At length he started up and exclaimed,

'It is horrible!--horrible--Johanna! Some one must have sought to take your uncle's life. See, here it is in his own handwriting--listen!' and he read aloud:

'God grant that my enemy's wicked plot may not succeed! Why did I let my gold get into such iniquitous hands, and place my life at the mercy of one more ferocious than a wild beast? He has, cunningly plundered me of my wealth--he has bound my tongue by an oath--and now he seeks to take my life in secret. But my money will not prosper in his unworthy hands--and accursed be the house over whose threshold his feet pass. There are human beings who can ruin others in all worldly matters, but mortal man has no power over the spirit when death sets it free.'

'What can this mean?' cried Frants, almost wild with excitement. Who is the mortal enemy to whom he alludes, but whom he does not name? Who has got possession of his house and his means? The same person, no doubt, who bound him by an oath to silence, and threatened his life in secret; who proclaimed to the world that he had drowned himself, and caused him to be buried like a suicide? Why was no other acquaintance called to recognize the body? We have no certainty that the drowned man was he. Perhaps his bones lie nearer to us than we imagine. Ha! old master, in my dream I heard you say, "Seek, and you shall find--why was I not put into consecrated ground?" Johanna! what do you think about that old lumber-room? There have been some mysterious doings there at midnight--there are some still--that floor is washed while we are sleeping. Before to-morrow's sun can rise I shall have searched that den of murder, from one end to the other.'

'Oh, dearest Frants, how wildly you talk; you make me tremble.'

But as Frants was determined to go, she sat down by the cradle to watch her sleeping child, while he took a light and proceeded to the workshop. There he seized a hatchet and crow bar, and thus provided with implements, he approached the door of the locked chamber.

'The room belongs to me,' said he to himself, 'who has a right to prevent me from entering it?'

To force the door by the aid of the iron crowbar, was the work of an instant, and without the slightest hesitation he went in, though it must be confessed he felt a momentary panic. But that wore off immediately, and he began at once to examine the place. Nothing appeared, however, to excite suspicion. There were some sacks of wood in a corner, and he emptied these, almost expecting to see one of them filled with the bones of dead men, but there was no vestige of anything of the kind. The floor seemed to be recently washed, for it was yet scarcely dry. He then began to take up the boards. At that moment he heard the handle of the door which led into the neighbouring house turning; holding the hatchet in one hand, and the light, high above his head, in the other, he put himself in an attitude of defence, while he called out:

'Has anyone a desire to assist me?'

Presently all was still. Frants put down his light, and began again hammering at the boards; almost unconsciously he also began to hum aloud an air which his old master used always to sing when he was engaged in finishing any piece of work. But he had not hammered or hummed long before the handle of the door was again turned. This time the door opened, and a tall, white figure slowly entered, with an expression of countenance as hellish as if its owner had just come from the abode of evil spirits.

'What, at it again, old man? Will you go on hammering and nailing till Doomsday? Must that song be heard to all eternity?' said a hollow but well-known voice--and Frants recognized with horror the ghastly-pale and wild-looking sleep-walker, who, with eyes open--but fixed and glazed--and hair standing on end, had come in his night-gear from his sleeping-chamber.

'Where didst thou lay my bones?' said Frants, as if he had become suddenly insane. 'Why was I not placed in my coffin?--why did I not enter a Christian burying-ground?'

'Your bones are safe enough,' replied the pallid terrible-looking dreamer, 'no one will harm them under my pear-tree.'

'But whom didst thou bury under my name--as a self-murderer, when thou didst fasten on me the stain of guilt in death?' asked Frants, astonished and frightened at the sound of his own voice, for it seemed to him as if a spirit from the other world were speaking through his lips.

'It was the beggar,' replied the wretched somnambulist, with a frightful contortion of his fiendish face, a sort of triumphant grin. 'It was only the foreign beggar to whom you gave your old grey cloak ... but whom I drove from my door that Christmas-eve.'

'Where *he* lies shalt thou rot--by *his* side shalt thou meet me on the great day of doom!' cried Frants, who hardly knew what he was saying. He had scarcely uttered these words when he heard a fearful sound, something between a shriek and a groan--and he stood alone with his light and his hatchet--for the howling figure had disappeared.

'Was it a dream,' gasped Frants, 'or am I mad? Away, away from this scene of murder--but I know *now* where I shall find that which I seek.'

He returned to Johanna, who was sitting quietly by the still sleeping child, and was reading the holy Scriptures.

Frants did not tell her what had taken place, and she was afraid to ask; he persuaded her to retire to rest, while he himself sat up all night to examine further the papers in the old Bible. The next day he carried them to a magistrate, and the whole case was brought before a court of justice for legal inquiry and judgment.

'Was I not right when I said that a coffin would come out of that house before the end of the year?' exclaimed the baker's wife at the corner of the street, to her daughter, when, some time after, a richly-ornamented coffin was borne out of Frants's house. The funeral procession, headed by Frants himself, was composed of all the joiners and most respectable artisans in the town, dressed in black.

'It is the coffin of old Mr. Flok,' said the baker's daughter, 'he is now going to be *really* buried, they say; I wonder if it be true that his bones were found under a tree in Mr. Stork's garden.'

'Quite true,' responded a fishwoman, setting down her creel, while she looked at the funeral procession.

'Young Mr. Frants had everything proved before the judge--and that avaricious old Stork will have to give up his ill-gotten goods.'

'Ay--and his ill-conducted life too, perhaps,' said the man who kept the little tavern near; 'if all be true that folks say, he murdered the worthy Mr. Flok.'

'I always thought that fellow would be hanged some day or other--he tried to cheat me whenever he could,' added the baker's wife.

'But they must catch him first,' said another; 'nothing has been seen of him these last three or four days.'

On Christmas-eve there sat a cheerful family in the late Mr. Flok's house near the canal. The child had quite recovered, and Frants, filling the old silver goblet with wine, drank many happy returns of the season to his dear Johanna.

'How little we expected a short time ago to be so comfortable now!' he exclaimed. 'Here we are, in our own house, which was intended for us by your kind uncle. I am no longer compelled to nail away alone at coffins until midnight, but can undertake more pleasant work, and keep apprentices and journeymen to assist me. My good old master's name is freed from reproach, and his remains now rest in consecrated ground, awaiting a blessed and joyful resurrection.'

The lumber-room with its fearful recollections was shut up. The outside of the house was painted anew--and the mysterious inscription on the wall, thus obliterated, never reappeared.

Frants had occasion one day, shortly after this favourable turn in their affairs, to cross the long bridge; and as he passed near the Dead-house for the drowned, he went up to the little window, saying to himself--'Now I can look in without any superstitious fears, for I know that my old master never drowned himself,--THAT foul stain is no longer attached to his memory; and his remains have at length obtained Christian burial.'

But when he glanced through the window he started back in horror, for the discoloured and swollen features of a dead man met his view, and in the dreadful-looking countenance before him, he recognized that of the murderer--Stork--who had been missing some time.

'Miserable being!' he exclaimed, 'and you have ended your guilty career by the same crime with which you charged an innocent man! None will miss you in this world except the executioner, whose office you have taken on yourself. I know that you had planned my death, but enemy as you were, I shall have you laid decently in the grave, and may the Almighty have mercy on your soul!'

Prosperity continued to attend the young couple--but the lessons of the past had taught them how unstable is all earthly good; the old family Bible--now a frequent and favourite study--became the guide of their conduct; and when their happiness was clouded by any misfortune, as all the happiness of this passing life must sometimes be, they resigned themselves without a murmur to the will of Providence, reminding each other of the watchman's song on that memorable night when all hope seemed to have abandoned them:

> 'Redeemer, grant Thy blessed help
> To make our burden light.'

THE FELON'S REVERIE

In a narrow cell sat one who was a prisoner for life. Around him were the four dingy walls, covered with great black characters, scratched thereon at sundry times with bits of charcoal: but there was no pleasure in reading these hieroglyphics, for they were the fruit of solitude and melancholy, whose heavy, heavy thoughts had thus expressed themselves. High up was placed the little window, the only connection with life, with nature, and with the heavens; but the black iron bars kept watch over that, and obscured the clear daylight. The links of his chain, round his hand and his foot, kept the prisoner bound in his dreary cage, but they could not fetter the soul's deep longing after liberty.

Days and years had passed in this gloomy cell. A charming, fresh summer's morning it was, when the door of this prison was first closed on him, and when he was told that Death alone should set him free. Here he had remained ever since; severed from the rest of mankind, shut up from them as if he had been a wild beast; and their farewell words to him had been--that Death alone was to be his deliverer. This was so dreadful a thought that he did all he could to drive it away. He worked diligently, he whistled, he sang, and he engraved strange names and figures on the walls. He frequently gazed up at the window, though he could only see through it a dead wall, but over that wall were the blue skies. He soon came to know every stone in the wall; he knew where the sun cast its streaks of light: where the little streams of water trickled down when it rained; there was more variety in the sky--it seemed to have compassion upon him, for sometimes the clouds were chased along by the wind; sometimes they assumed strange, fantastic shapes, and arrayed themselves in crimson and gold, like the gorgeous garb of royalty; and sometimes they hung in heavy, dark masses over the lofty wall--the boundary of his external world. But he saw no living things; and once, when a daring swallow rested for a few minutes on the outside ledge of his iron-barred window, he scarcely breathed, in his anxiety to enjoy the sight of it as long as possible.

Winter was his saddest time, for *then* the snow blocked up his little window, and intervened between him and the skies; then, too, it became so early dark, and daylight was so long of coming. He sang and whistled no longer; he worked, indeed, but not so diligently, for his tormentor--*thought*--had more power over him. During the short day he could partly escape it; but when it became dark--oh! what had it not then to recall to him! And the worst was, he was obliged to bear it all. He could have silenced another, but he could not hush the voice that spoke within himself. In vain he sought to banish remembrance; it *would* haunt him: so he dropped his head upon his hands, and listened.

And it spoke to him of the time when he was a little boy with rosy cheeks, who had never done harm to a living being, and who sat or lay in the bright sunshine, humming the song his mother had taught him. And that mother, who loved him so dearly, who worked for him during the day, and slept with him at night--well! She was dead, God be praised! 'Perhaps if she had lived,' said he to himself. No, no! Does he not remember well one day, when the little boy with rosy cheeks was coming from school, that he passed a blind old man who was begging, and holding out his hat in his hand, that he dived quickly into the hat, and caught up the pence some charitable persons had placed in it? No one saw him--no one knew that he had done this--why does he now remember it with such bitter regret?

His mother died, and a neighbouring family received the orphan kindly; consoled and caressed him, and he slept by the side of their dog. But they were very poor themselves, and could not maintain him long; therefore he was sent to other people, where some one paid a small board for him, and where he, the little stranger, was far from being well treated. He had too little to eat--and he stole food; therefore he was ignominiously turned away, and he fell among wicked people. They talked to him of the paths of virtue--but they followed vicious courses themselves, and he laughed at their admonitions. He grew older, and he went to be confirmed[7] in the House of God; and there he was admitted to the Holy Sacrament. The priest laid his hand with blessings on his head, and he there pledged his heart to God, and vowed to forsake all sin. How comes it that he now so distinctly remembers the solemn tones of the organ as he was leaving the church, and the large painting of the Saviour close by the altar, which he had turned to look at once more before he passed from the crowded aisle? He had never been in that church again to pray--alas! never.

He had, indeed, been there again--but it was on another and a reprobate errand--and *then* he was young at that time, and reflected less. Ah! *then*, too, he thought more of the young and beautiful girl who had knelt next to him at the altar, and with whom he had afterwards taken a quiet walk. On other evenings he was wont to spend his time with some wild, bad companions, and to join in their giddy mirth and mischievous sports; but that evening, their company wearied and disgusted him, and he followed the young girl to her father's house. He had now become an apprentice: but he was careless and idle: to sit hard at work did not suit his taste. And yet these were pleasant days when he looked back on them.

He became a journeyman, and was betrothed to his pretty friend of the Confirmation-day. She had gone into service, and was a hard-working, honest, well-principled girl; *he* continued to be idle. Often and often she entreated him to be more industrious, to seek work, and not to waste his time on riot and strife; and often he promised to reform. But his only reformation was, that he took more pains to conceal from her his bad habits. When he was sitting with her, and her anxious look rested upon his dull eyes, or his faded cheek, he felt that it was time to stop in his career of evil, and resolved to become a steady and respectable workman. But these good resolutions vanished when he left her presence. At length the evil spirit within him conquered; he wanted money, and stole a watch from a fellow-workman. Then the arm of the law seized him, never again to let him go.

After he had undergone the punishment awarded to his theft, he came, abashed and with downcast eyes, to his betrothed; but she had heard of his guilt. With bitter tears she reproached him for his conduct, and she forbade him ever again to show himself in her presence. He was furious at her reception of him, and left her, vowing to be revenged. Many wild schemes rushed through his brain:--now he determined to murder her; now, that she should also be dragged into disgrace. But one day he met her in the street, and her pale, tearful, melancholy countenance disarmed his wrath, and annihilated his plans of revenge.

And now, as the prisoner scrawls absently with that rusty nail on the wall, and his sunken eyes fill with warm tears, what is memory recalling to his saddened mind? Ah! is it not that short-lived time of early affection--is it not those sweet, calm features--those speaking eyes--that love, so true and so pure? Perhaps his fancy paints himself as an honest, industrious citizen, as a happy husband and father, with *her* by his side, and in a very different place from that dreary cell--in a comfortable home, enjoying all that he so madly threw away--love, happiness and respectability! But his thoughts wander on; he throws the nail away from him, and leans back, with arms folded across his chest.

He left the town and went into the country. There was a voice in his soul which urged him to reform. 'Return, return!' it said; 'return, for there is yet time!' But another voice also spoke--that of the demon which enslaved him; and that demon was--THE HABIT OF IDLENESS. Unhappily he then fell in with a depraved wretch--a villain experienced in crime--an escaped convict. They wandered about among the peasantry and begged; but every door was closed against his companion, with unmistakable signs of terror and distrust.

One summer night they had taken shelter in a stable, and he had fallen fast asleep. He was awakened by his comrade. 'Get up,' said he, 'men will give us nothing--the Lord must help us, therefore.' He thought the man alluded to some intended theft, and accompanied him without the least reluctance. They stole along the gardens and fences on towards the churchyard. He stopped his guide.

'What are we to do here? 'he asked, with uneasiness. 'You surely will not--'

'What?' asked the other, laughing.

'Oh, let the dead rest in peace!'

'Fool!' cried the convict, 'do you think I am going to meddle with the dead? Follow me!'

And he scaled the walls of the churchyard, and broke open the Gothic door of the church. Now he understood what his companion meant to do; but his heart beat as if it would have started out of his breast. As he went up the aisle, he felt as if he had lead in his shoes--as if the flooring held him back at every step--as if it were a whole mile to reach the altar. He had not entered the house of God since the day he had been there to take upon himself his baptismal vow, and dedicate his life to his Creator; and now--now he stood there to plunder! His hands trembled violently, as he held open the sack for his comrade, who cast into it the silver cups, the silver salvers, and everything that he could find of value; and had it not been for fear of his ferocious associate, he would assuredly have thrown down the sack and fled, for he thought that the picture of Christ over the altar looked earnestly and reproachfully at him. When his companion looked up from his sacrilegious work, and observed his eyes fixed, as it were, by some fearful fascination on the picture, he nodded to it in a scoffing manner, and then closed the sack, and left the church.

When they were out of it, the prisoner breathed more freely; and when they placed themselves on a tombstone to divide the booty, he received without hesitation the portion that his comrade chose to allot to him. They buried their treasure in the earth, and separated. But the massive altar-plate could not easily be disposed of. He was in want; he begged from door to door, but he was driven from them all; so he had again recourse to stealing. Since the night that he had been drawn into robbing the church, he had felt that he was an outcast from the whole world--an outcast from God himself. He knew that punishment was sure to overtake him, and he was miserable.

His companion in guilt was soon after arrested; he confessed all, and they were both imprisoned, and put to hard labour.

But he had not yet quite lost all hope. He determined to work in future for his daily bread. He came out of gaol a half-savage, half-frightened being--lonely and deserted--bearing upon him that brand of infamy which never more could be erased; but he had made up his mind to labour, and he went far away to seek for employment.

It was the harvest-time. God had blessed the fields, and there were not reapers enough to gather in the corn. No question was asked whence he came, but his services were immediately accepted. There was something in this display of the bounty of the Creator, in this activity, in this working in the free open air, that pleased him; for the first time in his life he toiled cheerfully. But the country people did not like him; his look was downcast and dark--he was rough and passionate, abrupt in speech, and he spoke little. After the farm-servants had one day proposed to him to go to church, and he had refused positively, but with an air of embarrassment, he was looked upon with great suspicion. There was but one face that always smiled at him, and that was the face of the youngest boy upon the farm. He had won the child's heart by having once cut out some little boats for him, and sailed them in the pond; and from that time the child always clapped his hands with joy when he saw him. It was so new, so delightful to him to be beloved, that he felt himself insensibly attracted towards the little creature. He indulged him in all his childish whims, carried him about in his arms, made toys for him, and seemed to feel himself well rewarded by the innocent child's attachment.

Thus passed the winter. Peace, hitherto unknown to him, was creeping into his heart; and when he stood in spring on the fields with the sprouting seeds, and heard the lark's blithe carol, a new light began to dawn on his benighted mind. One day, when he returned from the fields towards the farm-yard, his little friend ran up to him, jumping and playing. He stretched out his arms to the child, but in an instant he started back, pale and horror-stricken. His former associate stood before him, with a malignant smile upon his sinister countenance, and held out his hand to him, while he said, in a tone of bitter irony,--

'So, from all I hear, you are playing the honest man in the place! Excuse me for interrupting your rural content, but I have been longing so much for you.'

'Away, demon!' cried the unfortunate man. 'Go, go, and leave me in peace!'

'Not so fast!' replied the other, with a withering sneer. 'I have told the people of the farm who you are. Do you think I am going to lose so useful a comrade?'

At that moment the grandfather of the child came up, and when he saw the little boy in the arms of him whom he had just been told was a malefactor, he snatched him hurriedly away, in spite of the child's tears and cries; and applying many abusive epithets to the man, ordered him instantly to leave the farm. The disturber of his peace carried him off with him, while his fiendish laughter rang around!

See! the prisoner's chest is heaving with emotion. Hark! what deep sighs seem to rend his heart, while a few scalding tears are falling from his eyes! Of what is he dreaming now?

He sees himself, in the grey dawn of day, stealthily creeping along the hedges that surround the farm, to catch a glimpse of his little favourite. He beholds the infant's soft cheek wet with the tears of affection; he feels his tiny arms clasped lightly round his neck; the kind words of farewell ring in his ears; he listens again for the sound of the retiring little footsteps, as the child is leaving him, and sees the little hand waving to him a last adieu from the door of his mother's house. As he then threw himself down beneath the hedge on the dewy grass, and burst into tears, he now hides his face on his hard pallet, and sobs aloud.

But he has risen from that recumbent position. He wrings his hands, and his teeth chatter, in his solitary cell. What horror is passing through his mind? What agonizing remembrance has seized him, and is shaking soul and body, as the roaring tempest shakes the falling leaves? Let it stand forth from its dark concealment! In vain he presses his hands on his bloodshot eyes not to behold that scene--in vain he tries to close his ears against those voices--the blackest night of his gloomy prison cannot veil *that* picture, for it arises from the darkest depths of his inmost soul.

Listen how his evil-minded associate tempts him, and draws him on!

'Yon old man at the farm has plenty of money--ready money--do you hear? Do you think I lost my time there? His daughter and her husband are his heirs; they do not need his gold so much as we do. The old man sleeps in that low house near the larger one. It is but a step through the window, and we shall be rich for a long time.'

'But what if he should awake, and recognize us?' asked the prisoner, with much anxiety.

The other made a gesture which shocked him. He started back.

'No, no!' he cried, shuddering; 'no blood!'

His companion laughed.

'What matters it whether the old man dies a few days sooner or later? People have generally no objection to the death of those to whom they are to be heirs. And have you forgotten how roughly he spoke to you? How he abused you, and drove you away? At that time I am sure you thirsted for revenge. Besides, how are you going to live? Perhaps you think you may find some good-natured fool to take a fancy to you; but you forget that *I* like you too well to separate from you.'

Want, fear, revengeful feelings, got the better of him; but at night, when like two spectres they glided along the road, it seemed to him constantly as if some one saw him; and notwithstanding his companion's ridicule, he frequently looked back. And truly there was ONE who watched him, but not with any mortal eye. They opened the window, and got in one after the other, and easily found the old man's desk, which was in the next room. The robber's practised hand soon opened it, and he was about to take its contents, when the door of the bedroom was suddenly thrown back and rapidly shut, and the old man, who was still hale and strong, entered, armed with a thick cudgel. A short but furious struggle ensued; he remembered having seized him by the back of his neck with both his hands, and dragged him down on the floor; he remembered having heard some dull blows, that made him shiver with horror, and then having stood in breathless dismay by a dead body. The two criminals looked at each other with faces of ashy hue; then the most hardened kicked the corpse to one side, and went to secure the booty, while the prisoner opened the door of the sleeping-room to search it.

But--oh, anguish unspeakable! oh, avenging God!--who should spring forward to meet him, clinging to his knees and imploring his protection--who but his innocent, unfortunate little favourite! He started back, speechless and powerless; but when he beheld his comrade, without uttering one word, brandish his knife, he clasped the child with one arm in a convulsive embrace, and stretched out the other to defend him against the ruffian.

'Shall he be left to betray us both to-morrow?' mumbled the wretch. 'He must die, for your sake as well as mine.'

'Oh, let us take him with us!' prayed the other, in the deepest agitation, while he tried to keep off the knife, which, however, he did with difficulty, as the child held fast to his arm, and, in his terror at the murderous weapon, hid his little face on that breast where he had so often rested in happy confidence, his silver voice murmuring his childish love.

'You are mad,' said his companion. 'What should we do with the boy? Let go your hold of him, I say--we have no time to lose--let him go, or it will cost you your own life.'

The quivering lips of the miserable man had scarcely uttered a prayer to wait, at least, till he could withdraw, when the child was torn from him, and like a maniac he rushed away, sprang out of the window, threw himself upon the ground, and buried his head among the long damp grass. What a moment of agony! Such agony, that at the remembrance of it the prisoner groaned aloud, and dashed his head against the stone wall, then coiled himself up like a worm, as if he would fain have shrunk into nothing.

The dear-bought, blood-stained booty was divided, and the criminal associates separated. But suspicion fell upon them; they were pursued, and soon taken. On being carried before a magistrate, he denied it all; yet when he was placed by the dead body of the murdered child, guilt spoke in his stiff, averted head--in the tell-tale perspiration that stood on his brow--and in his clenched and trembling hands. He confessed, and implored to be removed, even to prison, from the harrowing spectacle. His accomplice was condemned to death, he himself to imprisonment for life.

There he was now, alone with the dreadful recollections of former days. The summer came and went, without bringing any other joy to him than that the sun's rays fell broader, and more golden in their gleams upon the wall outside that bounded his narrow view; and that now and then a bird would fly over it, quiver a few notes, then wing its flight away. That sight always awoke a voice in his heart that cried for 'Freedom--freedom!' But he would hush it with the thought, that he could not be happier were he at liberty than in his dungeon cell. At other times, he would take a violent longing to see a green leaf--only a single green leaf--or a corn-blossom from the fields, or a blade of grass. Ah! these were vain wishes! When winter came, and the sun and the daylight forsook him so soon, he was still more gloomy, for he could not sleep the whole of the long, long night, and the phantoms that haunted him were terrific.

Once--it was a Christmas night--he was reflecting on all the joy that was abroad in the world, and he thought if it would not be possible for him to pray. Then long-forgotten words returned to his lips, and he faltered out, 'Our Father, which art in heaven!'--but *then* he stopped.

'God is in heaven,' thought he, 'how can He condescend to hear the sigh that arises from the hell within my breast? No, no--it is but mocking Him for *me* to pray!'

Days and years had gone by since the prisoner had inhaled the breath of the fresh balmy air, had beheld the extended vault of heaven, or wandered in the bright, warm sunshine; at length the spirit had exhausted the body. He lay ill and feeble, and death was near. Then was the narrow door of his dungeon opened, and he was removed to a more cheerful place--to a place where the blessed air and light were freely admitted, and where the voices of human beings were around him. But their compassion came too late. Earnestly did he entreat them to let him see a minister of the Gospel; and when one came, he poured out the misery of his soul to him. He listened with the deepest attention while the holy man discoursed about Him, who, in His boundless love, shed His own blood to wash out the sins of mankind, and in whose name even the darkest and most guilty criminal might dare to raise his blood-stained hands in prayer. How consoling were not these precious words to him, 'My God and my Saviour! With what an earnest longing he waited to be permitted to participate in that solemn rite which, by grace and faith, was to unite him to that Redeemer! And how he trembled lest the lamp of his mortal life should be extinguished before the first spark of that sacred flame was lighted, which was to be kindled for an endless eternity!

The time that his repentant spirit so thirsted for arrived. And when he had partaken of the holy communion, and tears of penitent sorrow had streamed over his burning cheeks, peace--long unknown--returned to his weary heart, and his gratitude found vent in thanksgivings and prayer.

'Oh!' he exclaimed, as he looked out of his open window, 'it is spring, my friends--I feel that it is spring, beautiful spring!'

'Yes,' replied the superintendent of the hospital, 'it is spring; even the old tree by the wall is green. See here, as I passed it, I broke off this budding twig for you;' and he placed the little green branch in the hand of the dying man.

'Oh!' said he, with a melancholy smile and a tear in his eye, 'that old, decayed, withered tree--can it put forth new leaves--fresh, green, sweetly scented as these? May I not then venture to hope that the Almighty may call forth a new life from me in another world? Oh, that such may be His will!'

And with the green bough--the proof of God's power and goodness in his hand, and with his Redeemer's promise on his lips, he passed to his everlasting doom, in the blessed hope that he also might touch the hem of his Saviour's garment, and hear these words of life--'Son, thy sins be forgiven thee!'

MORTEN LANGÈ A Christmas Story BY HANS CHRISTIAN ANDERSEN

Each midnight from the farthest Thule, to isles the South Sea laves, To exercise themselves awhile the dead forsake their graves; But when it is the Christmas time they stay much longer out, And may in the churchyard be seen, then, wandering about; And as they dance their merry rounds, the rattling of their bones Produces, 'midst the wintry blasts, somewhat unearthly tones. Poor things! For them there's neither wine, nor punch, nor supper there, The icicles are all they have, and a mouthful of fresh air. When shines the moon strange forms are seen, tall spectral giants some: Such sights as these might even strike a chattering Frenchman dumb. Scoff not at my poor hero, then, though once in a sad fright-- He is a most discreet young man, and Morten Langè hight.

One Christmas night the fates ordained a journey he must make, So, for despatch, 'twas his resolve a horse and sledge to take. Dark was the hour, and in the skies the ranks of stars looked pale, While from a tower near hooted owls, as in a German tale. And Morten Langè, by-the-by, was not unlearned, for About Molboerne's exploits[8]--also the Trojan war, 'Octavianus,' Nisses, Trolls, Hobgoblins well he knew, And all about 'the spectre white,' whose story is so *true*. Too soon the sledge stood at the door, with many a jingling bell; But ah! these sounds to his sad ears seemed like his funeral knell. Yet, though the snow-flakes fell around, of them he took no heed, But like a British runaway pair, he started at full speed. He passed a regiment of old trees, whitened from top to toe, And soon he gained an open plain, where nought he saw but snow. Like Matthison's 'Gedichte,' 'twas very, very cold, But still our hero tried to think that he was warm and bold. He did not care to gaze about, and so half-closed his eyes; Yet, spite of this precaution--lo! a curious sight he spies: A muster of the Elfin-folk enjoying a gay spree, The men were just five inches high, the women only three; And though 'twas at the chill Yule-time, when cold reigns over all,

In clothes of flimsy cobwebs made, they capered at their ball; The ancient dames, however, wore some more substantial gear, For of bats' wings their shawls were formed--but, softly--what comes here?

Twelve harnessed mice, with trappings grand, fit for a monarch's own, They draw a car of fairy work, where a lady sits alone. It stops, and Morten Langè sees the lady getting out-- 'Heav'n help me now! Heav'n help me now!' he sighed, for he dared not shout. 'I'm no poltroon, and yet I feel the blood within my veins Is freezing fast.' In mortal fear, his cold hand dropped the reins; Then stooping to recover them out of the sledge he fell, And with it scampered off the horse, whither he could not tell. He felt that his last hour was come, all helpless as he lay-- And with such thoughts upon his mind he fainted quite away.

At length, when consciousness returned, and when his swoon was o'er, He heard a fearful buzzing sound, that frightened him still more. What had he done to be exposed that night to such alarms? A troop of demons round him thronged--one imp secured his arms. Another seized his lanky legs, another caught his head-- And powerless to resist them then, away with him they sped. They carried him to some strange place, flames shone upon the walls, Into another fainting-fit, half-dead with fright, he falls, But when the pains of death seemed past, and trembling he looked round, He saw that in the other life a sad fate he had found. The vaulted roof was black with smoke, and awful was the heat; The devils stood with naked arms--he dared not scan their feet. One held a hammer in his hand, and threatening, waved it nigh, And in a burning furnace there, red flames were flashing high. Soon guessed our hero where he was, and set himself to kneel, And lustily for mercy prayed--but they laughed at his appeal.

Then to his side an angel came, benignant was her smile, And holding out her small white hand, she said to him the while; 'Well, Heaven be praised, you're better now! But why are you afraid?' Shaking with fear in every limb, in a faint voice he said: 'Oh, angel! 'tis not death I dread, but help me out of hell!' The angel laughed: 'You're in good hands--you ought to know us well. This is the smithy--from your sledge thrown out upon the ground, Lying alone amidst the snow half-frozen you were found; And I'm no angel, bless your heart! I'm Annie, don't you see?' Rubbing his eyes, and staring round, up Morten jumped in glee; And that he soon forgot his fright 'tis needless to declare-- The roasted goose, the foaming ale, and other Christmas fare, As might be guessed, put all to rights--and Annie by his side At supper sat, that Christmas night, as Morten Langè's bride.

Note by the Translator

The ghost-story alluded to--'Den hvide Qvinde' (The White Woman)--is to be found in Thiele's collection of Danish 'Folkesagn.' This spectre is said to haunt some old ruins near Flensborg. Two soldiers, long, long ago, were keeping their night-watch on the ramparts of the castle; one of them left his post for a short time, and when he was gone the other sentry was approached by a tall female figure in white, who accosted him thus:--'I am an unblessed spirit, who have wandered here for many hundred years, and have never found rest in the grave.' She then informed him that under the walls was buried an immense treasure, which could only be found by *three* men in the world, and that he was one of the three. The soldier, fancying his fortune made, promised to obey her in all things, and received her command to be on the spot the following midnight. In the meantime the other sentinel had returned to his post, and had overheard what the spectre had related to his comrade. He said not a word, however, but the next night he went to the appointed place, and concealed himself in some recess close by. When the soldier who was to dig for the treasure arrived, with his spade and other implements, the white spectre appeared to him, but knowing that he was watched, she put off the *digging* till another night. The man who had intended to act as a spy was taken suddenly ill as soon as he got home; and feeling that he was about to die, he sent for his comrade, confessed that he had watched him, implored him to avoid witchcraft and supernatural beings, and recommended him to consult the priest, who was a wise and good man.

The soldier took his advice, and laid the matter before the priest, who directed him to do the spectre's bidding, only taking care that *she* should be the first to touch the treasure. The man accordingly met the ghost at the appointed time and place, and she showed him the spot where the treasure was deposited; but before taking it up, she told him that one half would be for him, and the other half must be divided between the church and the poor. But the demon of avarice had entered into his heart, and he exclaimed: 'What! shall I not have the whole of it?' Scarcely had these words passed his lips, than the spirit uttered a fearful thrilling cry, and disappeared in a blue flame over the castle moat. The soldier was taken ill, and died three days afterwards. The story became noised about, and a poor student determined to try his luck. He repaired to the old castle at midnight, saw the wandering 'White Woman,' told her his errand and offered his services. But she informed him that he was not one of the chosen three, and could not assist her, and that the walls would thenceforth stand so firmly, that hand of man should never overthrow them. However, she promised at some future time to reward him for his good intentions.

One day, long after, when he happened to be loitering near the old castle, and thinking with compassion of the fate of the restless spirit who haunted it, he stumbled over something; and, on stooping to see what it was, he discovered a large heap of gold, of which he forthwith took possession. As foretold by the spectre, the walls of the castle are still standing, and the story goes, that whenever any portion of them has been overthrown, it has always been raised again by invisible agents during the night. Matter-of-fact people assert that the locality of this ghost tradition is a *hill*, not a *castle*.

A TALE OF JUTLAND BY S. S. BLICHER

I had often beheld the highest hill in Denmark, but had not hitherto ascended it. Frequently as I had been in its neighbourhood, the objects of my journeys had always required me to turn off in another direction, and I was thus obliged to content myself with seeing at some distance the Danish Schwarzwald; and as I passed on, to cast a hurried glance down the valleys to the charming lake, dotted with green leafy islets, and which winds, as it were, round jagged tongues of land. At length I overcame all obstacles, and resolved to devote two days to a pleasure-trip amidst this much-admired scenery. My cousin Ludwig, who had just arrived from the capital, agreed to accompany me.

The morning was clear and warm, and gave the promise of a fine evening, but shortly after mid-day there gradually arose in the south-west a range of whitish clouds tinged at the sides with flame-colour. My cousin did not notice them; but I, who am experienced in the signs of the weather, recognized these indications of thunder, and announced to him 'that the evening would not be as fine as the morning.' We were riding exactly in such a direction that we had these clouds opposite to us, and could, therefore, perceive how they kept rising higher and higher, how they became darker at the base, and how they towered like mountains of snow over the summit of the hill. Imagination pictured them to us like the Alps of Switzerland, and we tried to fancy ourselves in that mountainous country; we saw Schreckhorn, Wetterhorn, and the Jungfrau; in the valleys between the clouds we pictured to ourselves the glaciers; and when a solitary mass of cloud, breaking suddenly, sank down, and seemed to mingle with the mountain chain, we called it an avalanche which would overwhelm villages and scattered chalets with everlasting snow. We continued, absolutely with childish pleasure, to figure to ourselves in the skies the majestic scenery of the Alps, and were quite wrapt up in our voluntary self-deception, when the sudden roar of thunder awoke us from our fantastic dreams. Already there stretched scarcely the thinnest line of light in the heavens above us, and the wood which lay before us seemed as if in a moment enveloped in a thick mist by the fast-falling rain. We had been too long dilatory, and now we rode as hard as possible to reach the nearest village; and we were soaked to the skin before we got to Alling, where we sought shelter under an open gateway.

The owner of the place, an elderly farmer, who seemed a sort of half-savage foreigner to us, received us with old Danish hospitality; he had our horses taken to his stable, and invited ourselves into his warm parlour. As soon as he observed our drenched condition, he offered us garments belonging to his two sons to wear while our own wet ones were dried by the blazing hearth. Joyfully did we avail ourselves of his kind proposal; and in a room upstairs, called the best apartment, we soon made the comfortable change of apparel, while laughing and joking at our unexpected travestie. Equipped as peasant lads in their Sunday's clothes, we shortly after rejoined the family. Our host was much amused at the change in our outward men, and warmly extolled our homely appearance, while his two daughters smiled, and stole sly glances at us--

'Blushed the Valkyries, whilst they turned and laughed.'

The coffee-urn stood ready on the table, surrounded by china cups; the refreshing beverage, amply provided with brown sugar and rich unadulterated cream, poured out and handed by one of the pretty daughters, speedily restored genial heat to our chilled blood; and then the father of the family thought it time to inquire the names, occupations, and places of abode of his unexpected guests.

Meanwhile the thunderstorm had passed away; the sun smiled again in the cloudless west; far away to the east, indeed, could still be heard the distant whistling and rattling of the winds, but where we were all was mild and tranquil. The spirits of the storm had folded their dripping wings, and the raindrops sparkled like diamonds upon every leaf and flower. The evening promised once more to resemble the morning in beauty.

'And now for the ascent of the mountains!' we exclaimed to each other.

'But your clothes?' interrupted the farmer. We hastened into an outer room, where the other fair daughter was busy drying them; but, alas! they were still quite damp, and she said she feared she could not promise that they would be in a fit state to be put on for at least an hour; and then it would probably be too late to enjoy the view from the top of the hill, as the ascent, proceeding from where we were at that moment, would take, perhaps, another hour. What was to be done? The good-natured countryman helped us out of our dilemma.

'If you are not ashamed of wearing the boys' clothes,' said he, 'why should you not keep them on?'

'That is a capital idea,' we both replied, and thanking him for the offer, as we shook hands with him cordially, we asked him where we could find a guide.

'I will myself be your guide,' he said, as he took from a corner a juniper-stick for each of us. We then lost no time in commencing our journey, and still more gaily than before, for we were much amused at our masquerade, especially my cousin, who seemed to feel no small admiration for himself in the rustic blue frock-coat, ornamented with silver buttons--the jack-boots--and the head surmounted by a high-crowned hat.

'I sincerely wish,' said he, 'that we could fall in with some other travellers up yonder; that would be great fun.'

Our guide laughed, and hinted that he would not be able to talk like the peasantry.

'Yes, I can though,' said my cousin, who immediately began to speak in the Jutland dialect, to the infinite diversion of the worthy Peder Andersen who, however, found still another stumbling-block to the perfections of the pretended peasant--namely, that his nice white hands would betray him.

'I can put them in my pocket' ('A ka put em i e Lomm),' cried my gay cousin, who was determined to admit of no drawback to his assumed character.

Presently we reached the river Gudenade, which is here tolerably wide, and has rather a swift current. We crossed in a boat something like a canoe, and then entered on quite another kind of a country; for here commenced the moorlands, covered with heather whose dark tints formed a strong contrast to the bright green on the east of the river. We had yet a good way to walk, and as the heather, which almost reached up to our knees, was still wet with rain, we had good reason to be grateful to our long boots. We approached the wood--a wood of magnificent beech-trees--which appeared to me here doubly beautiful, standing out, as it did, against so dark a background. Amidst sloping dales the path wound always upward; but the thickness of the foliage for a time deprived us of any view. At last we emerged from the wood, and found ourselves upon the open summit of the mountain.

When I hear delightful music, or witness an interesting theatrical representation, I always like to enjoy it for a time in silence. Nothing acts more unpleasantly, jars more on my feelings, than when any one attempts to call my attention to either. The moment the remark is made to me, 'How beautiful that is!' it becomes less beautiful to me These audible outbursts of admiration are to me like cold shower-baths, they quite chill me. After a time, when I have been left undisturbed, and by degrees have cooled in my excitement, I am willing to exchange thoughts and mingle feelings with those of a friend, or of many friends; indeed, I find desire growing within me to unburden, if I may so express it, my overladen mind. It is thus that a poet utters his inspirations: at the sweet moment when he conceives his ideas, they glow within him, but he is silent; afterwards he feels constrained to give them utterance; the voice or the pen *must* afford the full heart relief. Our guide's anxiety to please was a dreadful drawback to my comfort, for, with the usual loquacity of a cicerone, he began to point out and describe all the churches that could be described from the place where we were standing, invariably commencing with, 'Yonder you see.' I left my cousin to his elucidation of the country round, and, wandering to some little distance, I sat down where I could *see*, without being compelled to *hear*.

When Stolberg had finished translating Homer into German, he threw down his pen, and exclaimed, despondingly, 'Reader, learn Greek, and burn my translation!' What is a description of scenery but a translation? Yet the most successful one must be as much inferior to the original as the highest hill in Jutland is lower than the highest mountain in Thibet. Therefore, kind reader, pardon my not describing to you all I saw. *What* I saw I might, perhaps, be able to relate to you, but scarcely *how* I saw it. My pen is no artist's pencil; go yourself and take a view of it! But you, who perhaps have stood on the summit of the Brochen, or of St. Bernard, smile not that I think so much of our little mountain! It is the loftiest that I, or perhaps many of my readers, have beheld; therefore, what is diminutive to you is grand to us.

I was startled in my meditations by a thump on my shoulder--it was from my cousin, who was standing behind me. He informed me that our guide had gone home at least half-an-hour, and that I had been sitting for a long time perfectly motionless, without giving the slightest sign of life. He told me, moreover, that he was tired of such solemn silence, and I must really awaken from my fit of abstraction.

'And at what have you been looking that has engrossed your thoughts so much?' he added.

'The same as you have been looking at,' I replied: 'Air, and earth, and water.'

'Well, cast your eyes down now towards the lake,' said he, handing me his spy-glass, 'and you will see that there are some strangers coming over this way.'

I took the glass and perceived a boat a little way from the shore, which seemed to be steering straight across the water; it was full of people, and three straw bonnets indicated that there were women among them. My cousin proposed that we should await their coming, although it would be late before we should reach our quarters for the night at Alling. As the evening was so charming, I willingly consented; we could not have wished a finer one. The sun was about to set, but it seemed to us to sink more slowly than usual, as if it lingered to behold longer the beauty of earth when tinged with its own golden rays. The winds were hushed, not a blade of grass, not a leaf was stirring. The lake was as a mirror, wherein were reflected the fields, the groves, the houses that lay on its surrounding sides, while here and there, in the valleys towards the west, arose a thin column of smoke from dwellings that were concealed by trees. But if in the air all was silence, sounds enough proceeded from the earth. Feathered songsters carolled in the woods behind us, and before us the heath-lark's love-strains swelled, answering each other from the juniper-bushes. From the bulrushes which grew on the margin of the lake was heard the quacking of the wild ducks; and from a greater distance came the plashing of the fisherman's oar, as he was returning to his home, and the soothing tones of his vesper hymn.

The sun had now sunk below the horizon, and the bells that rang from many a church for evening prayer, summoned the weary labourer to rest and sleep. The heavy dews of night were already moistening the ground, and its mist was veiling the woods, the lake, and the sloping banks. Now broke upon the ear the cheering yet plaintive music of wind instruments. It seemed to come nearer and nearer, and must undoubtedly have proceeded from the boat we had observed putting off from the opposite shore. When the music ceased, we could distinctly hear the voices of the party in the boat, and presently after the slight noise made by their landing. We stood still for a few minutes, expecting to see them ascending the hill, but soon perceived that, on the contrary, they were going in another direction, for the sound of the voices became fainter and fainter, and was lost at last apparently among the woods to the west. Had it not been that the airs they had played were of the newest fashion, we might have fancied it a fairy adventure--a procession of woodland elves, or the bridal of the elf king himself.

The shades of night were falling around. Here and there a star glimmered faintly in the pale-blue skies. In the north-west was visible a red segment over the horizon, where the king of day was wandering beneath, on his way to lighten another hemisphere. Now, all was still; only at a distance on the heath we heard the plover's melancholy note, and beneath us, on the lake, the whizzing of the water-fowls' wings as they skimmed its darkened surface. 'Let us go homewards now!' cried my cousin. 'Yes, home!' I replied. But we had not gone far before we both stopped at once with a 'Hush! hark!' From the margin of the wood, through which we had just come, issued suddenly the sound of harmonious voices, singing as a duet a Tyrolese air. There is something indescribably charming and touching in this unison of voices, especially in the open air, when the sweet tones seem to float upon the gentle breeze; and now, at the calm evening hour, when the surrounding hills were awakened from the deep repose into which they had just subsided, the sweet tones had the effect of the nightingale's delightful song. My cousin seized my hand and pressed it, as if to entreat that I should not, by any exclamation, disturb his auricular treat. When the vocalists ceased, he sighed deeply. I gazed in astonishment on him; he was in general so gay, and yet at that moment tears actually stood in his eyes! I attributed to the mighty enchantment of music, the power of softening and agitating the hardest and the lightest heart, and I remarked this to him.

'Ah, well!' he replied, 'the human breast is like a sounding-board, which, although untouched, yet gives an echo when certain chords are struck.'

'You are right,' I said; 'as, for instance, the story of the tarantula dance.'

He sighed again, and said gravely,--

'But such chords must be connected with peculiar events--must awaken certain recollections--yes'--he took my hand, and pointing to the trunk of a tree which had fallen, we placed ourselves on it--'yes, my friend, yon air recalls to me a souvenir which I have in vain tried to forget. Will you listen to the story?'

'Tell it,' I said, 'though I can partly guess what it must be.'

It was on such an evening as this (he continued), about two years ago, that, accompanied by a friend, I had gone on a little tour of pleasure to Lake Esrom. We remained sitting a long time on a fallen tree before we could prevail on ourselves to wend our way homewards, so charmed were we with the beauty of the scenery and of the evening. We had just arisen when a Tyrolese air--the very one you and I have recently heard--sung delightfully as a duet, attracted our attention. It came from the side of the lake, but the sounds appeared to be gradually approaching nearer. We soon heard the plashing of oars, which kept time to the music, and shortly after we saw a boat making for the part of the shore where we were. When the song was ended, there was a great deal of talking and laughing in the boat, and the noise seemed to increase the nearer they came to the shore. We now saw distinctly the little skiff and its merry freight. 'Lay aside your oars!' said one; 'I will steer you straight in to the land.' They did so. 'I know a quicker way of making the land,' cried another, as he sprang up, and striding from gunwale to gunwale, set the boat rocking frightfully. 'Be quiet! be quiet!' roared a third; 'are you mad? The fool will upset the boat!' 'You shall have a good ducking for that,' said the madcap, swaying the boat still more violently. Then came shouts of laughter mingled with oaths; in the midst of the uproar a loud voice called out, 'Be done. I tell you! Fritz cannot swim.'

But it was too late--the boat was full of water--it upset. Happily it was only a short way from the shore. In one moment they were all silent; we heard only the splashing and hard breathing of those who were swimming. There were six of them. Presently one of them cried, 'Fritz! Fritz! come here! take hold of me!' Then cried another, 'Fritz, come to me!' And then several voices shouted, 'Fritz! Fritz! where are you?' Two of them had by this time reached the shore, and they stood looking anxiously at those who were still swimming in the lake. One of them began counting, 'Three, four!' Then crying in a voice of extreme consternation, '*One* is wanting!' he sprang again into the water, and the other instantly followed his example!

My friend and I could no longer remain mere spectators of this scene; we threw off our coats and were speedily in the water, searching with the party for their lost friend. We thought he must be under the boat; therefore we all gathered round the spot where it lay keel upwards, and the best swimmer dived beneath it. In vain! he was not there. But at a little distance, amidst the reeds, one of us observed something dark--it was the missing Fritz! He was brought on shore; but he was lifeless. Zealously, anxiously, did we try all means of restoring him; they were of no avail. It was decided that he should be carried to the nearest house. A plank, which had formed one of the seats of the boat, and which had floated to the shore, was taken up; he was placed upon it, and they carried him towards the road. We followed them mechanically. What a contrast to their late boisterous mirth was their present profound silence! We had not proceeded far, when one of the foremost of the bearers turned round and exclaimed, 'Where is Sund?' We all looked back, and beheld the unfortunate madcap who had caused the accident half-hidden behind a tall bush, stuffing his pockets with pebbles.

'He will drown himself,' said the person who had just spoken; 'we must take him with us.'

They stopped, and my companion and I offered our assistance to carry the body, whilst two of the party went to their repentant friend. The way to the house to which the drowned man was to be carried lay through a wood. It was so dark amidst the trees that we were close upon two female figures, dressed in white, before we observed them,

'Good Heavens!' cried the foremost of the party; 'if it should be Fritz's betrothed! She said she would probably come to meet us.'

It was indeed herself. You may imagine the painful scene: first, her horror at meeting us carrying a drowned man, and then her agony when she found out that the unfortunate victim was the one dearest to her on earth; for she could not be deceived, as she knew them all. She fainted, and her companion caught her in her arms as she was falling to the ground.

What was to be done? My friend and I hastened to the assistance of the ladies, while the other gentlemen hurried on with the inanimate body to the house, which was at no great distance. I ran to the lake, and brought back some water in my hat; we threw a little on her face, when she soon came to herself again, poor thing!

'Where is he?' she screamed; 'oh! where is he? He is not dead--let me go to him--let me go!' She strove to rise and rush forward.

'Leave her, kind gentlemen,' said her companion, as she threw one arm round her waist, and with the other pressed her hand to her heart. 'Thanks--thanks for your assistance, but do not trouble yourselves further; I know the way well.'

We bowed and stood still, while she hastened on with her poor friend; and as they went we could hear the sorrowful wailing of the one, and the sweet soothing tones of the other. Having received no invitation we had no right to follow them, and we sought our carriage, both deeply impressed by the melancholy catastrophe which we had involuntarily witnessed.

We were not acquainted with any member of the party, nor were we able to hear anything of them. In vain we searched all the newspapers, and conned over all the announcements of deaths in their columns; there never appeared the slightest reference to the unfortunate event I have just mentioned, nor did we ever hear it alluded to in society. We should certainly, after the lapse of some time, have looked upon the whole affair as a freak of the imagination--a phantom scene--had we not played a part in it ourselves. It did not make so light an impression on me, however; you will think it strange, perhaps absurd, but I actually was partially in love! Love has generally but one pathway to the heart--the eyes; it took a by-path with me--through the ears. It was so dark that I had not seen the young lady's features; I had only heard her voice. But, ah! what a voice it was! So soft--*that* does not describe it; so melodious--neither does that convey an idea of what it was. I can compare it to nothing but the echo of tones from celestial regions, or to the angel-voices which we hear in dreams. Her figure was as beautiful as her voice--graceful and sylph-like. If you have ever been bewitched in a night vision, you will be able to comprehend my feelings. I saw her, and I did not see her. Her slight form with its white drapery looked quite spiritual in the dim light, and reminded me of Dido in Elysium, floating past Æneas, who was still clothed in the garb of mortality.

'Of whom are you speaking?' I asked. 'Of the friend?'

'Of course,' he replied; 'not of the widowed girl, as I may call the other.'

'I do not see anything so very extraordinary in what you have been telling me,' I said. 'When it is almost dark, fancy is more easily awakened; everything wears a different aspect from what it does in the glare of day--objects become idealized, and sweet sounds make more impression on the mind, while imagination is thus excited. But is this the end of your drama?'

'No; only the first act,' he replied. 'Now comes the second.'

The summer passed away; winter came, and it too had almost gone, when I happened to attend a masquerade at one of the clubs. For about an hour I had been jostled among the caricaturists, and was becoming very tired,--and falling into sombre reflections upon the illusions of life, and the masks worn in society to conceal people's real characters from each other, when my attention was attracted by twelve shepherds and shepherdesses in the pretty costume of Languedoc, who came dancing in, hand in hand. The orchestra immediately struck up a French quadrille, and the French group danced so gracefully that a large and admiring circle was formed round them. When the quadrille was over, the circle opened, and the shepherds and shepherdesses mingled with the rest of the company. One of the shepherdesses, whose charming figure and elegance of motion had riveted my attention, as if by a magic power drew me after her. I followed wherever she went, until at last I got so near to her that I was able to address her.

'Beautiful shepherdess!' I said in French, 'how is it that our northern clime is so fortunate as to be favoured by a visit from you and your lovely sisters?'

She turned quickly towards me, and after remaining silent a few moments, during which time a pair of dark eyes gazed searchingly at me,

'Monsieur,' she replied in French, 'we thought that fidelity had its true home in this northern clime.'

'You have each brought your lover with you,' I said.

'Because we hoped that they would learn lessons of constancy here,' was her answer.

'Lovely blossom from the banks of the Garonne!' I exclaimed, 'who could be inconstant to you?'

'There is no telling,' she continued, gaily. 'You are paying me compliments without knowing me. You call me pretty, yet you have never seen *me*. It must be my mask that you mean.'

'Your eyes assure me of your beauty,' said I; 'they must bear the blame if I am mistaken.'

Just at that moment another dance commenced; I asked the fair shepherdess to be my partner, and consenting, she held out her hand to me. We took our places immediately. It was then that a recollection came over me of having heard her sweet voice before. I thought that I recognized it--yes! Surely it could be no other's than hers--my fairy of Esrom Wood! But I was determined to be certain of the fact. I said nothing, however, while we were dancing. The dance seemed to me very short, and at the same time endless.

I interrupted him somewhat uncivilly with--'At any rate your story seems endless.' He continued, however.

After the dance was over I conducted her to a seat, and placed myself by her side.

'It strikes me,' I remarked in Danish, 'that T have once before heard your voice, but not on the banks of the Garonne--'

'No,' she replied, interrupting me, 'not there, but perhaps on the borders of Lake Esrom?'

A sweet feeling at that moment, as it were, both expanded and contracted my breast. It was herself--the Unseen! She must also have remarked my voice, and preserved its tones in her memory.

'A second time we meet,' I sighed, 'without beholding each other. This is really like an adventure brought about by some magician's art; but, oh! how I long for the moment when you will no longer hide that charming countenance.'

She laughed slightly; and there was something so sprightly, musical, and winning in her laugh, while her white teeth glistened like pearls under her mask, that I forgot what more I was going to say. She, however, began to speak.

'Why should I destroy your illusion? Leave our adventure, as you call it, alone; when a mystery is solved it loses its interest. If I were to remove my mask, you would only see the face of a very ordinary girl. Your imagination gallantly pictures me beautiful as some Circassian, or some Houri; let me remain such in your idea, at least till the watchman cries the hour of midnight, and wakes you from your dreams.'

'All dreams are not delusive,' I said. 'They often speak the truth,' I added; 'yet sometimes one is tempted to wish that truths were but dreams; as, for instance, the very unfortunate event which was the occasion of our first meeting.'

She looked surprised, while she repeated--

'Unfortunate? Ah! true. You probably never heard--' At that moment one of the shepherds ran up, and carried her off hurriedly to a quadrille which was just forming.

I was following the couple with my eyes, when my sister tapped me on the arm and asked me to dance with her, as she was not engaged. Mechanically I took my place in the quadrille, the same in which my *incognita* was dancing, and mechanically I went through the figures until she had to give me her hand in the chain. I pressed it warmly, but there was no response. Ashamed and angry, I determined not to cast another glance at her; and resolutely I turned my head away. The quadrille was over, and once more I found myself constrained to look at her. But she was gone--the shepherds and shepherdesses had all disappeared. Whether they had left the ball, or--what was more probable--had changed their attire, I saw them no more. In vain at the supper-table my eyes wandered over all the ladies, to guess, if possible, which was the right one. Many of them were pretty; many had dark eyes and white teeth; but which of all these eyes and teeth were hers? It was by the voice alone that I could recognize her; but I could not go from the one to the other, and ask them to speak to me. And thus ended the second part of my drama.

'Now, then, for the third act,' said I, with some curiosity.

'For that,' he replied, 'I have waited in vain, above a year and a day.'

'But do you not know her name?' I asked.

'No.'

'Or none of the party of shepherds and shepherdesses?'

'I found out shortly after that I knew two of the shepherds; but of what use was that to me? I could not describe my shepherdess so that they could distinguish her among the twelve; they mentioned a dozen names, all equally unknown to me. That gave me no clue; to me she was both nameless and invisible.'

I could not help smiling at my usually-gay cousin's doleful countenance.

'You are laughing at me,' said he. 'Well, I don't wonder at it. To fall in love with a girl one has never seen is certainly great folly. But do not fancy that I am going to die of despair. I only feel a sort of longing come over me when I think of her.'

The singers had now come so near that we could hear their conversation. After a few moments my cousin whispered to me that he knew one of them by his voice, and that he was an officer from Copenhagen. In another minute they made their appearance. There were three of them, all dressed as civilians, but the moustaches of one showed that he was a military man. My cousin squeezed my arm, and whispered again--

'It is he, sure enough; let us see if he knows me.'

We rose, and stood stiffly, with our caps in our hands. They nodded to us, and the officer said--

'Put your hats on, lads. Will you earn a shilling for something to drink, and help to erect our tent?'

We agreed to his proposal, and at his desire we joined two men in fetching, from a cart near, the canvas and other things required to put the tent up; also cloaks, cushions, baskets with provisions, and bottles of wine, benches for seats, and a wider one for a table. When our services were no longer needed, the officer held out some money to me, which, of course, I would not receive. My cousin also refused payment; whereupon he swore that we should at least take something to drink, and, filling a tumbler from his flask, he handed it to my cousin, who received it with a suppressed laugh.

'What are you grinning at, fellow?' said the officer; but, as my cousin carried the tumbler to his lips, he exclaimed--

'Your health, Wilhelm!'

The individual thus addressed started back in astonishment, while his two companions peered into our faces. My cousin burst into a fit of laughter; and the officer, who now recognized him, cried, laughing also,--

'Ludvig! What the deuce is all this? and why are you equipped in that preposterous garb?'

The matter was speedily explained; the three travellers expressed much pleasure at meeting us, and pressed us so cordially to join their party, and stay the night with them, that we at length acceded to their request.

One of the officer's companions was a young, handsome, and very fashionable-looking man; he was extremely rich, we understood, therefore they called him *the merchant*, and they would not tell us his name, or if that were his *real* position in society. The other introduced himself to us with these words:

'Gentlemen, of the respectable peasant class! my name here in Jutland is Farniente. My agreeable occupation is to do nothing--at least nothing but amuse myself.'

There was a great deal more joking among our hosts, and then we presented each other in the same bantering way, after which we all adjourned to the tent, where we wound up with a very jovial supper. At midnight the merchant reminded us that we had to rise next morning with the first rays of the sun, and that it was time to retire to rest. We made up a sort of couch, with cushions and cloaks, and on it we five faithful brothers stretched ourselves as best we might. The other four soon fell asleep. I alone remained awake; and when I found that slumber had fled my pillow, rose as quietly as possible, and left the tent.

All around was still as the grave. The skies were without a cloud, but of their millions of eyes only a few were now open, and even these shone dimly and feebly, as if they were almost overcome by sleep. The monarch of light, who was soon to overpower their fading brightness, was already clearing his path in the north-east. It is not the darkness, still less the tempest, that renders night so extremely melancholy; it is that deep repose, that corpse-like stillness in nature; it is to see oneself the only waking being in a sleeping world--one living amidst the vast vaults of the grave--a creature trembling with the fearful, giddy thought of death and eternity. How welcome then is any sound which breaks the oppressive silence of that nocturnal solitude, and reminds us that human beings are about to awaken to their daily round of occupation and pleasure--and, it must be added, of anxiety and trouble! How cheerful seems the earliest crowing of the cocks from the nearest huts, rising almost lazily on the dusky air! The drowsy world was beginning to move; and after a time I discerned faint, sweet tones proceeding from the direction of the wood. I listened attentively, and soon became convinced that it was music--the music of wind instruments--which I heard. To me music is as welcome as the first rosy streaks of morn to the benighted wanderer, or a glimpse of the brilliant sun amidst the gloom of a dark wintry sky.

The sweet sounds ceased, and I began to ponder whether it might not have been unearthly strains which I had heard--whether they might not have come from the fairies who perhaps dwell amidst the surrounding glades, or among the wild flowers that enamelled the sloping sides of the hills. The music, however, was certainly Weber's, and the question was, whether the elfin people had learned the airs from him, or he from them. I returned to the tent, where the still sleeping party produced a very different and somewhat nasal kind of music.

'Gentlemen! gentlemen!' I shouted, 'there are visitors coming.'

My cousin was the first to awaken, then the officer, who sprang up, and immediately endeavoured to arouse the other two.

'The ladies will be here presently,' he said; 'get up both of you.'

'They are too early,' groaned one; 'I have not had half my sleep.'

'Let them wait outside the tent till I am ready,' said Farniente. 'Good night!'

The rest of us, however, went towards the wood to meet the three ladies, who were making their way to our temporary domicile, preceded by two musicians playing the horn, and two youths bearing torches, the latter being the sons of a clergyman in the neighbourhood, at whose house the ladies had slept. Observing the peasant costume of my friend and myself, the ladies asked who we were, and were told by the military man that we were two soldiers of his regiment, who, being in the adjacent village, had assisted in putting up the tent.

'Lads,' said he, addressing us in a tone of command, 'can you fetch some water for us from the nearest stream, and get some wood for us to boil our coffee? I will go with you.'

'No, no, sir--that would be a shame,' said my cousin, in the Jutland dialect; 'we will bring all that is wanted ourselves.'

When we returned to the tent it was broad daylight; Farniente had been compelled to vacate his couch of cloaks, and in his lively way was greeting the fair guests with 'Good morning, my three Graces.' The officers told us, aside, that two of the ladies were his sisters, and were about to tell us more, when a waltz on the turf was proposed by Farniente, who seized one of the ladies, whom he called Sybilla, as his partner. *The merchant* danced with another, to whom it appeared he was engaged, and the officer took his youngest sister. Their hilarity was infectious, and my cousin dragged me round for want of a better partner, whereupon the fair Sybilla, who had observed our dancing, remarked that we were 'really not at all awkward for peasant lads.'

While they were taking their coffee afterwards, during which time we stood respectfully at a little distance, my cousin whispered to me how much he admired the lieutenant's youngest sister, who was indeed extremely pretty. He had not hitherto heard her voice, but he could not help seeing that she looked attentively--even inquisitively at him. By Farniente's request, the ladies handed us some coffee, after having done which they made some remarks upon us to each other in German. At that moment my cousin let his coffee-cup drop suddenly to the ground, and standing as motionless as one of the trees in the wood, he fixed his eyes upon the youngest girl with a very peculiar expression, which called the deepest blushes to her cheek.

We all looked on in surprise, but I began to suspect the truth. Farniente was the first to speak.

'Min Herre!' said he, 'it is time that you should lay aside your incognito, for it is evident that you and this lady have met before.'

My cousin had by this time recovered his speech and his self-possession. He went up to the young lady, and said:--'For the first time to-day have I had the happiness of seeing those lips from which I have twice heard a voice whose accents delighted me. In that voice I cannot be mistaken, so deep was the impression it made upon me. Dare I flatter myself that my voice has not been quite forgotten by you?'

Catherina--that was her name--replied with a smile,--

'I have neither forgotten your voice nor your face, though last time we met you were a Spanish grandee.'

'What is all this?' exclaimed the officer; 'old acquaintances--another masquerade!'

'We are now truly all partaking of rural life,' said Farniente; 'so come, you two peasants, and place yourselves with the fair shepherdess and us.'

We joined the circle, and after our names having been told, my cousin, leading the conversation to Lake Esrom, and the events which took place on its banks, asked Catherina how her poor friend had taken that sad affair, and if she had ever recovered her spirits?'

'Oh yes, she has,' replied Catherina; and pointing to the young lady who was engaged to *the merchant*, 'there she is!'

My cousin started, and said, in some embarrassment, 'It was a sad event, but--'

'Not so very sad,' cried *the merchant*, interrupting him, 'for the drowned man returned to life. He was no other than myself.'

'God be thanked!' exclaimed my cousin, sincerely rejoiced at the pleasant intelligence. 'That is more than we *then* dared to hope. But what became of the poor foolish madcap who first upset the boat and then wished to drown himself?'

'Here he is,' said Farniente, pointing to himself; 'and as I once thought I might be promoted to the dignity of court jester, I took a wife, and there,' bowing to Sybilla, 'sits the fair one who has undertaken to steer my boat over the dangerous ocean of life.'

The morning mists by degrees cleared away from the wooded valleys and the hill-encircled waters; the larks had ended their early chorus, and the later songsters of the grove had commenced their sweet harmonies; all seemed joy around, and I looked with pleasure at the gay group before me. Never had the cheering light of day shone upon a circle of more contented human beings, and among them none were happier than Ludwig and his recently-found shepherdess, whose countenance beamed in the radiant glow of dawning love.

Six months have passed since then, and they are now united for this world and for that which is to come.

THE SECRET WITNESS BY B. S. INGEMANN

In the year 1816 there lived in Copenhagen an elderly lady, Froken F----, of whom it was known that she sometimes involuntarily saw what was not visible to anyone else. She was a tall, thin, grave-looking person, with large features, and an expressive countenance. Her dark, deep-set eyes had a strange glance, and she saw much better than most people in the twilight; but she was so deaf, that people had to speak very loudly to her before she could catch their words, and when a number of persons were speaking at the same time in a room, she could hear nothing but an unintelligible murmur. A sort of magnetic clairvoyance had, doubtless, in the somewhat isolated condition in which she was placed, been awakened in her mind, without, however, her being thrown into any peculiar state. She only seemed at times to be labouring under absence of mind, or to have fallen into deep thought, and then she was observed to fix her eyes upon some object invisible to all others. What she saw at those moments were most frequently the similitude of some absent person, or images of the future, which were always afterwards realized. Thus she had often foreseen unexpected deaths, and other unlooked-for fatal accidents. As she seldom beheld in her visions anything pleasing, she was regarded by many as a bird of ill omen, and she therefore did not visit a number of families; those, however, who knew her intimately both respected and loved her. She was quiet and unpretending, and it was but rarely that she said anything, unsolicited, of the results of her wonderful faculty.

She was a frequent guest in a family with whom she was a great favourite. The master of the house was an historical painter, and his wife was an excellent musician. The deaf old lady was a good judge of paintings, and extremely fond of them; also, hard of hearing as she was, music had always a great effect upon her; she could add in fancy what she did not hear to what she did hear; she had been very musical herself in her youthful days, and when she saw fingers flying over the pianoforte, she imagined she heard the music, even when anyone, to dupe her, moved their fingers back and forwards over the instrument, but without playing on it.

One day she was sitting on a sofa in the drawing-room at the house of the above-mentioned family, engaged in some handiwork. The artist had a visitor who was a very lively, witty, satirical person, and they were standing together near a window, discoursing merrily; they often laughed during their conversation, and the tones of their voices seemed to change, occasionally, as if they were imitating some one, whereupon their hilarity invariably increased, which, however, was far from being as harmless and goodnatured as mirth and gaiety generally were in that house.

When the visit was over, and the artist had accompanied his friend to the door, and returned to the drawing-room, the old lady asked him who had been with him.

He mentioned the name of his lively friend, whom, he said, he thought she knew very well.

'Oh, yes, I know him well enough,' she replied; 'but the other?'

'What other?' asked the painter, starting.

'Why the tall man with the long thin face, who stood yonder; he with the dark, rough, uncombed-looking hair, and the bushy eyebrows--he who so often laid his hand on his breast, and pointed upwards, especially when you and your merry friend laughed heartily.'

'Did you ever see him before?' inquired the artist, turning pale. 'Did you observe how he was dressed, and if he had any peculiar habit?'

'I do not remember having ever seen him before; as to his dress, it was very singular, much like that of an old-fashioned country schoolmaster.' And she described minutely his long frock-coat, with large buttons and side-pockets, and his antiquated boots, that did not appear to have been brushed for a very long time. 'The peculiar habit you speak of,' she added, 'was probably the manner in which he slowly shook his head, when he seemed to differ in opinion from you and your other guest; in my eyes there was something noble and striking in this movement, there was an expression of pain or sadness in his countenance, which interested me; it was particularly observable when he laid his right hand on his breast, and raised his left hand upwards, as if he were solemnly affirming something, or calling God to witness to the truth of what he said. Nevertheless, I remarked with surprise, that I scarcely saw him open his lips. It was of course impossible for me to hear what you were all talking about.'

The terrified artist became still paler--he tottered for a moment, and was obliged to lean on the back of a chair for support. Shortly after he seized his hat and hurried out of the house. The individual whom the old lady had so graphically described had been a friend of his in youth, but with whom he had been on bad terms for the last two years, and whom he had not seen lately.

The whole conversation with his amusing visitor had been about this very man. They had been engaged in a laughable and, at the same time, merciless criticism of his character, and appearance, and had been turning into ridicule every little peculiarity he had; his very voice they had mimicked, and in their facetious exaggeration, had not only made a laughing-stock of his person and manners, which were indeed odd, but had attributed to him want of heart and want of judgment, which latter sentence they based upon his somewhat peculiar taste, and a kind of dry, pedantic, schoolmaster tone in conversation, from which he was not free.

'That old maid is mad--and she has made me mad, too,' mumbled the artist, pausing a moment when he had gained the street. '*He* certainly was not there--we do not meet any longer. She never saw him before. There is something strangely mysterious in this matter--perhaps it bodes some calamity. But, whether she is deranged--or I--or both of us, I have wronged him--shamefully wronged him--and I must see him, and tell him all.'

He stepped into a bookseller's shop, and asked to look at a Directory. After about half-an-hour's walk he entered a house in a small back street, and ascending to the third story, he rang at a door. A girl opened it, and, in answer to his inquiries, told him that the person he asked for was ill, and could not see anyone.

'But I must see him--I must speak to him,' cried the painter, almost forcing himself in.

He was then ushered into a darkened room, where he found his poor friend of bygone days looking pale and emaciated, lying perfectly still upon a sofa, in his old grey frock-coat and soiled boots. The kind anxiety with which the unexpected visitor asked about his health seemed equally to surprise and please the invalid.

'You!' he exclaimed, '*you* here! Do you still take any interest in me? Have you any regard left for me? I did you shameful injustice two years ago, when I saw your great masterpiece; and had not an enthusiastic word for what I have though, often since, thought of with the greatest admiration. Nay, within this very last hour I have wronged you, though in quite a different manner. I was dreaming of you, and I fancied you were speaking of me with scorn and derision--pulling me to pieces in a jesting conversation with a very satirical person, who vied with you in ridiculing me, and in mimicking all my oddities.'

'Forgive me--oh, forgive me! you dreamed the truth,' cried the painter, in great agitation, while he threw himself down by the sick man's couch, and embraced his knees.

An explanation ensued between the two friends who had so long been estranged from each other--mutual confessions were made--old feelings were revived in the hearts of both--and an entire reconciliation immediately took place. The unusual emotion, and the surprise at the event related to him, did not, as might have been expected, increase the illness of the nervous and debilitated invalid; on the contrary, the meeting with his former friend appeared to have had a good effect on his health, for in the course of a few weeks he had quite recovered.

The old lady's qualifications as a seer, or rather her strange faculty of beholding, to others invisible, apparitions, had been productive of good; but it was such an extraordinary revelation, agreeing so entirely with what both the reconciled friends knew to be the truth, that they could only look upon it as a proof of the reality of what was then beginning to be so much talked of--the magnetic clairvoyance.

They continued unalterable friends from that time. From that time, also, the artist felt an involuntary horror at ridiculing the absent, or making or listening to any censorious remarks upon them; he always fancied that the injured party might be standing *as a secret witness* by his side, with one hand on his breast, and the other raised in an appeal to that great Judge, who alone can know what is passing in every heart and every soul.

AGNETE AND THE MERMAN BY JENS BAGGESEN

Agnete she was guileless.
She was beloved and true,
But solitude, it charm'd her,
And mirth she never knew--
She never knew--
She made the joy of all around
Yet never felt it too.

Over the dark blue waves,
Agnete, gazing, bends,
When lo! a merman rising there
From ocean's depths ascends;
Up he ascends.
Yet still, Agnete's bending form
With the soft billows blends.

His glossy hair, it seemed as spun
Out of the purest gold,
His beaming eye, it brightly glow'd
With warmest love untold--
With love untold!
And his scale-cover'd bosom held
A heart that was not cold.

The song he sang Agnete,
On love and sorrow rang;
His voice it was so melting soft,

So sadly sweet he sang--
Sadly he sang.
It seemed as if his beating heart
Upon his lips it sprang.

'And hearken, dear Agnete!
What I shall say to thee--
My heart, oh! it is breaking, sweet!
With longing after thee!
Still after thee!
Oh! wilt thou ease my sorrow, love,
Oh! wilt thou smile on me?'

Two silver buckles lay
Upon the rocky shore,
And aught more rich, or aught more bright,
No princess ever wore,
No, never wore.
'My best beloved,'--so sang he--
'Add these unto thy store!'

Then drew he from his breast
A string of pearls so rare--
None richer, no, or none more pure
Did princess ever wear--
Oh! ever wear.
'My best beloved,' so sang he,
'Accept this bracelet fair!'

Then from his finger drew he
A ring of jewels fine--
And none more brilliant, none more rich,
Midst princely gems might shine;
'Here, here from mine.

My best beloved,' so sang he,
'Oh, place this upon thine!'

Agnete, on the deep sea
Beholds the sky's soft hue,
The waves they were so crystal clear,
The ocean 'twas so blue!
Oh! so blue!
The merman smiled, and thus he sang,
As near to her he drew:--

'Ah! hearken, my Agnete,
What I to thee shall speak:
For thee my heart is burning, love,
For thee, my heart will break!
Oh! 'twill break!
Say, sweet, wilt thou be kind to me,
And grant the love I seek?'

'Dear merman! hearken thou,
Yes, I will list to thee!
If deep beneath the sparkling waves
Thou'lt downward carry me--
Take thou me!
And bear me to thine ocean bow'r
There, I will dwell with thee.'

Then stoppeth he her ears,
Her mouth then stoppeth he;
And with the lady he hath fled,
Deep, deep beneath the sea!
Beneath the sea!
There kiss'd they, and embraced they,
So fond, and safe, and free!

For full two years and more,
Agnete, she lived there,
And warm, untiring, faithful love
They to each other bear;
Such love they bear.
Within the merman's shelly bower
Are born two children fair.

Agnete--she sat tranquilly.
And to her boys she sang;
When hark! a sound of earth she hears,
How solemnly it rang!
Ding--dong--dang!
It was the church's passing bell
In Holmé Vale that clang.

Agnete, from the cradle,
Springs suddenly away,
She hastes to seek her merman dear,
'Loved merman, say I may--
Say--Oh say,
That I, ere midnight's hour, may take
To Holmé's church my way?'

'Thou wishest ere the midnight
To Holmé church to go?
See then that thou, ere day, art back
Here, to thy boys below--
Go--go--go!
But ere the morning light return
Come to thy sons below!'

He stoppeth then her ears,

Her mouth then stoppeth he;
And upwards they together rise
Till Holmé Vale they see.
'Now part we!'
They part, and he descends again
Beneath the deep blue sea.

Straight on to the churchyard,
Agnete's footsteps hie:
She meets--O God! her mother there,
And turns again to fly.
'Why--O why?'
Her mother's voice her steps arrests
Thus speaking with a sigh:--

'Oh hearken, my Agnete,
What I shall say to thee,
Where has thy distant dwelling been
So long away from me?
Away from me!
Say, where hast thou, my child, been hid
So long and secretly?'

'O mother! I have dwelt
Beneath the boundless main,
Within a merman's coral bower,
And we have children twain,
Beneath the main.
I came to pray--and then I go
Back to the deep again!'

'But hearken thou, Agnete,
What I to thee shall say--
Here thy two little daughters weep

Because thou art away;
By night, by day,
Thy little girls bemoan and grieve;
With them thou'lt surely stay?'

'Well--let my daughters small
For me both grieve and long,
My ears are closed--I cannot hear
Their cries yon waves among!
Oh! I belong
To my dear sons, and they will die
If I my stay prolong.'

'Have pity on thy babes--
Let them not pine away!
Oh! think upon thy youngest child
Who in her cradle lay!
With them oh stay!
Forget yon elves, and with thine own,
Thy lawful children stay!'

'Nay, let them bloom or fade--
The two--as Heav'n may will!
My heart is closed--their cries no more
Can now my bosom thrill--
Oh! no more thrill!
For now my merman's sons alone
All my affections fill.'

'Alas! though thou canst thus
Thy smiling babes forget;
Yet think upon their father's faith,
Thy noble lord's regret,
The fate he met!

As soon as thou wert lost to him
His sun of joy was set.

'Long--long he search'd for thee,
He went a weary way;
At last from yonder shelving rock
He cast himself one day--
One dismal day.
His corpse upon the pebbly strand
In the dim twilight lay!

'And here--'twas not long since--
His coffin they did bring;
Ha! list, my daughter, hearest thou?
The midnight bells they ring!
Ding--dong--ding!'
Away her mother hastens then
As loud the church bells ring.

Agnete, o'er the church-door
Stepp'd softly from without,
When all the little images
They seem'd to turn about;
Round about.
Within the church, the images
They seem'd to turn about.

Agnete gazes on
The altar-piece so fair;
The altar-piece it seem'd to turn,
And the altar with it there.
All where'er
Her eye it fell within the church,
Seem'd turning, turning there!

Agnete, on the ground
She gazed in thoughtful mood,
When lo! she saw her mother's name
That on a tomb-stone stood.
There it stood!
Then, sudden from her bursting heart,
Flow'd back her chill'd life's blood.

Agnete--first she stagger'd back,
She fainted, then she fell.
Now may her children long in vain
For her they loved so well.
Oh, so well!
Now, neither sons nor daughters more
To her their wants may tell.

Ay! Let them weep, and let them long,
And seek her o'er and o'er!
Dark, dark, are now her eyes so bright,
They ne'er shall open more!
Oh, never more!
And crush'd is now that death-cold heart,
So warm with love before.

A WAKING DREAM

He sat alone. It was not twilight, it was night, deep, dark night. He had extinguished the lamp, for he wished that all around him should be gloomy as his own sad thoughts. Even the pitiful glimmering light, which was cast by the fire in the stove on the objects near it, was disagreeable to him, for it showed him a portion, at least, of the scene of his bygone happiness. His bitter sorrow seemed to have petrified all his faculties, and entirely blasted his life; he did not appear to reflect, he only felt. The deep sighs that every now and then burst from his compressed lips were all that gave sign of existence about him. That agitated tremor, those wild lamentations, those burning tears,--the glowing look which griefs volcano casts forth, lay hidden amidst the ashes of mute and agonized suffering.

But a few years before he had been the most hopeful of lovers; and somewhat later, the happiest of husbands and of fathers. Now all--all was lost! Death had stretched forth his mighty hand and taken his treasures from him; blow after blew had fate thus inflicted on his bleeding heart. He--the strong man--the high-minded--the richly-endowed--sat there like a lifeless statue, without purpose, without motion, without energy: all had been swept away in the earthquake which had engulphed the happiness of his home, and he had not power to raise a new structure upon the ruins of the past.

While he was sitting thus, a momentary blaze in the fire showed him the portrait of his departed wife, which hung against the wall. How many recollections the sight of it awakened! Oh, how distinctly he remembered the day when that painting had been finished for him! It was a short time before his marriage; he was gazing on it in an ecstasy of delight, when the lovely original cast her beaming eyes on him and whispered, 'Do you really think it beautiful? Is it so beautiful that when I become old and grey-headed, you may look at my picture and remember your love, your feelings for me, when we were both young?' And when he assured her, that for him she would always be young, she replied so sweetly, 'Oh, I am not afraid of becoming old by your side; it will be so delightful to have lived a long life of love with you!'

Alas! he was still young, but he had to wander through perhaps a long, long life alone. How had he beheld her last? She was lying in her coffin--young and lovely, but pale and motionless. And he--who still breathed and felt--he it was who had clung in despair to that coffin--he who, with a breaking heart, had laid her dark hair smoothly on her marble-white cheek, had pressed his lips for the last time on her cold forehead, had folded her transparent hands and bedewed them with his tears, and had laid his throbbing head on that so lately beating heart, which never, never more would thrill with sorrow or with joy. But who could describe that depth of grief, that rending of the soul, that agonizing convulsion of the heart, when the last farewell look on earth--the long, eager, parting look--was taken, and the head was raised from the harrowing contemplation of these beloved features, which were soon to be snatched and hidden from his gaze! Then despair seized upon him, and his grief could find no relief in tears.

In these heart-breaking recollections his spirit was long absorbed; at length he pressed his hands on his aching temples, burst into a flood of tears, and exclaimed:

'Oh, thou whom I loved so truly! hast thou indeed forsaken me? Can it be possible that thou hast dissevered thyself from my soul! Oft have I dreamed that thou wert harkening to my lamentations, that thou wert lingering by my side, and soothing my sorrow! But it was fancy--cheating fancy! Thou who didst feel so much affection for me--thou who wert never deaf to my prayers--hast thou heard me, and yet not answered me? How often during the sad weary night have I not called upon thee! See--I stretch forth my arms and embrace only the empty air--I gaze around for thee, but am left in oppressive solitude. Oh, if thou *canst* hear me, beloved spirit! if it be possible that thou canst hear me--come, oh come!' His voice was choked by tears.

At last, when the water mist had passed from his eyes, removing, as it were, a veil from before them, he gazed wearily on the darkness around, and perceived a faint ray of light, which gradually seemed to become clearer. At first he thought it was the moon casting its uncertain gleams through the window; but the light seemed to extend itself. The corner of the room opposite to him seemed illumined by a pale, tremulous lustre that spread down to the floor. His heart beat violently as he gazed intently at the miraculous light. By degrees it assumed something like a shape, an airy, transparent figure, clad in a shining garment that glittered like the stars of heaven; and when it turned its countenance towards him, he recognized the features of her he had lost, but radiant in celestial peace and glory. Her clear eyes, which were fixed upon him, beamed with an expression of indescribable benignity.

The deep grief that had oppressed his spirit gave place to a wonderful, a mysterious feeling of holy calmness which he had never before experienced.

'Oh, speak!' he entreated softly, as if he were afraid to disturb the beautiful apparition, and holding his clasped hands beseechingly towards it--'Oh let me hear that voice, the echo of whose dear accents still lives in my heart! Hast thou taken compassion on me?'

'Didst thou not call me?' replied the apparition in a faint, subdued tone, yet so full of tenderness and affection that it seemed to inspire him with new life. 'Hast thou not often called me? I could no longer withstand thy supplication. The sorrows and sufferings of earth have lost their bitterness and their sting for those who have become heavenly spirits--those who have seen the Omnipotent face to face; but thy grief touched my heart even in the midst of blessedness. I could not be happy whilst thou wert wretched. Often have I hovered around thee, often lingered by thy side, often wafted coolness to thy burning brow; and when thy sadness would seem to be somewhat soothed, I have lain at thy feet, and contemplated thy beloved countenance. I was by thee when thou didst lean weeping over my coffin, and in an agony of woe didst cling to that body whence my soul had fled. Oh! how much I wished then that thou couldst look up at me, and know how near I was to thee! Oh! how willingly I would have embraced thee, had the Almighty permitted me! I was also with thee when our beloved infant lay in its last earthly struggle. My dying child called for me, and the heart of the mother yearned to respond to that call which had reached her, even when surrounded by the happiness of eternity, I came down to earth to answer it. Like an airy shadow, I glided through the garden paths in the still summer night, and all the plants and the flower exhaled their sweetest fragrance to salute me, for they felt that I had come from a better world. And Nature spoke to me with its spirit voice, and besought me to consecrate its soil with my ethereal step. The dark elder-tree and the blushing rosebush made signs to me, asking me if I remembered how often they had shed their perfume around us, when you and I, wrapped in our mutual happiness, used to wander in the soft evenings, arm in arm--heart answering heart--eye meeting eye--through the verdant alleys and flower-enamelled walks; but I could not linger over these sweet remembrances, I passed on to watch the death-bed of the little innocent who longed so for its mother. And when thou, my beloved! overcome by affliction, let thine aching head sink in helpless sorrow on its couch, our child lay, peaceful and joyous, in my embrace, and ascended to heaven with me to pray for thee. Oh, dearest one I how canst thou think that death has power to sever hearts that have once been united in everlasting love!'

He listened in mute and breathless ecstasy to these words, which sounded as the softest melody to his enraptured ear. When the voice ceased, he stretched forth his arms towards the beloved shade, and said beseechingly:

'Forgive me, angel of Paradise--forgive me! I feel now that the happiness of heaven is so great that nothing mortal can compare with it. Yet for my sake thou hast left awhile this inconceivable felicity, and deigned to assuage my grief, and to speak balm to my heart. Thanks, blessed spirit--thanks! My path shall no longer be gloomy--my life no longer lonesome!'

'Thou wilt sigh no more--thou wilt no longer weep?' asked the spirit, with a radiant smile.

'Thou shalt be my guardian angel, blessed spirit!' he replied, in deep emotion.

'God be thanked!' ejaculated the spirit in holy joy. It waved its shadowy hand to him, and as it seemed to turn to move away, its airy robe sparkled luminously for a moment; it then glittered more and more faintly, till it looked like the twinkling of some distant star.

Then earth-born wishes seized again upon *his* heart.

'Alas;' he cried, as he made an involuntary movement towards the vanishing shadow, 'shall I, then, never behold thee more in this world?'

A holy light passed over the scarcely defined features of the spirit, while it replied, as if from afar--

'Yes! once more--but only once. When thy last hour approaches--when the bitterness of death is passed--then shalt thou tell those that watch by thy couch, and who, incredulous, will deem thy words the raving of delirium--then shalt thou tell them that a messenger from a glorious world is standing by thy side. That messenger will be me. I shall come to kiss the last breath from thy pale quivering lips, to gladden the last glance of thy closing eyes, and, after the heart's last pulsation, to receive thy parted soul, and be its guide to the realms of endless happiness, where I now await thee.'

He listened and bowed his head. When he raised it--all was dark and empty. He went to the window, and looked out upon the dazzling snow, and up to the brilliant star-lit heavens, and prayed in sadness, but with earnest devotion.

He lives to perform his duties, to do good to his fellow-creatures, to serve his God. He is never gay nor lively; but he is tranquil and content. He loves quiet and solitude. He loves in winter to lose himself in meditation while gazing on the calm, cold face of nature; and in summer to loiter in silence, till a late hour at night, amidst his garden's sweetly-scented walks. He is a lonely wanderer on the earth; yet not quite so lonely as he is thought to be, for he is often soothed by delightful dreams, and then he smiles happily, as if in his visions he had been consoled by the presence of a beloved being.

If his soul sometimes ventures humbly to indulge in the wish that it might soon enter into death's peaceful land, none can tell; his silent aspirations are known to none--to none but *Him* who sees into the deepest recesses of the human heart.

THE CONFESSIONAL BY CHRISTIAN WINTHER

In the Magdalene Church at Girgenti[9] preparations had been made for a grand festival. It was adorned, as usual on such occasions, with red tapestry and flowers. The hour of noon had struck, the workmen had left the church, and there reigned around that deep, solemn stillness which, in Catholic places of worship, is so appropriate and so imposing.

Two gentlemen, who conversed in a low tone of voice, were pacing up and down the long aisle that runs along the northern side of the building, and seemed to be enjoying the shade and coolness of the church, as if it had been a public promenade. The elder was a man of about thirty years of age, stout, broad-shouldered, and strongly built, with a grave countenance, in which no trace of passion was visible: this was Don Antonio Carracciolio, Marquis d'Arena. The other, who seemed a mere youth, had a slender, graceful figure, an animated, handsome face, and dark eyes, soft almost as those of a woman--which wandered from side to side with approving glances, as if he had some peculiar interest in the interior of the sacred edifice. And such he certainly had; for he was the architect who had planned the church and superintended its erection. He was called Giulio Balzetti, and had only lately returned from Rome. Suddenly they stopped.

'I shall entrust you with a secret, which I think will amuse you, Signor Marquis,' said the younger man, in the easy intimate tones in which one speaks to a friend at whose house one is a daily visitor--'a secret with which, I believe, no one is acquainted but myself. You see the effects of acoustics sometimes play us builders strange tricks where we least expect or wish them. Chance, a mere accident, has revealed to me, that when one stands here--here upon this white marble slab--one can distinctly overhear every syllable, even of the lowest whisper, uttered far from this, yonder, where you may observe the second last confessional; while, in a straight line between this point and that, you would not be sensible of any sound, were you even much nearer the place. If you will remain standing here, I will go yonder to the confessional in question, and you will be astonished at this miracle of nature.'

He went accordingly, but scarcely had he moved the distance of a couple of steps, when the Marquis distinctly heard a whisper, the subject of which seemed to make a strong impression upon him. He stood as rigid and marble-white as if suddenly turned to stone by some magician's wand; while the painfully anxious attention with which he listened, and which was expressed in his otherwise stony features, gave evidence that he was hearing something of excessive importance. He did not move a muscle--he scarcely breathed--he was like one who is standing on the extreme verge of an abyss, into which he is afraid of falling, and his rolling eyes and beating heart alone gave signs of his violent agitation.

In a very few minutes the young architect came back smiling, and called out from a little distance, 'I could not manage to make the experiment, for some one was in the confessional--from the glimpse I got, a lady closely veiled--but, Heavens! what is the matter with you?'

The only answer which the Marquis gave the Italian was to place his finger on his mouth, and he continued to stand motionless. After a minute or two he drew a deep sigh. The statue passed out of its speechless magic trance, and returned again to life.

'It is nothing, dear Giulio!' said he, in a friendly tone. 'Do not think that I am superstitious; but I assure you this mysterious and wonderful natural phenomenon has taken me so much by surprise, that it has had a strange effect on me. Come, let us go! I shall recover myself in the fresh air,' he added, as he took Balzetti's arm, and led him to the promenade on the outside of the town.

The two gentlemen walked up and down there for about an hour, when the Marquis bade the young man adieu, saying, at the same time, 'Tomorrow, after the festival is over, will you come out as usual to our villa?'

At a very early hour the next morning the Marquis entered his wife's private suite of apartments. The waiting-maid, who just at that moment was coming into the anteroom by another door, started, and looked quite astounded.

'Did your lady ring?' asked the Marquis.

'No, your excellency!' replied the woman, curtseying low and colouring violently.

'Then wait till you are called,' said the Marquis, as he opened the door of the dressing-room, which separated the sleeping-room from the antechamber.

As he crossed the threshold he was met by his lovely young wife, attired in a morning-gown so light and flowing, that it looked as if it must have been the one in which she had arisen from her couch. The Marquis stopped and stood still, as if struck with his wife's extreme beauty. He did not appear to observe the uneasiness, the inward tempest of feelings that, chasing all the blood from her cheeks, had sent it to her heart, and caused its beating to be too plainly visible under the robe of slight fabric which was thrown around her.

'You are up early this morning, Antonio!' said the young Marchioness, in a scarcely audible tone of voice, with a deepening blush and a forced smile. 'What do you want here?'

'Could you be surprised, my Lauretta? Light of my eyes!' said the Marquis, in the blandest and most insinuating of accents, 'could you be surprised if I came both early and late? And yet, dearest, this morning my visit is not to you alone. You know to-day is the feast of the Holy Magdalene, and a great festival in the Church. I have taken it into my head to usher in this day by paying my tribute of admiration to the glorious Magdalene of Titian, which you had placed in your own sleeping apartment. Will you permit me?' he asked, very politely, as with slow steps, but in a determined manner, he walked towards the door.

'Everything is really in such sad disorder there,' said his young wife, with a rapid glance through the half-open door; 'but ... go, since you will. I shall begin making my toilette here in the mean time.'

And he went in.

'How charming,' he cried, in a peculiar tone of voice--'how charming is not all this disorder! This graceful robe thrown carelessly down--these fairy slippers! There is something that awakens the fancy, something delicious in the very air of this room! All this is absolutely poetry.'

His searching look fastened itself upon the snow-white couch, the silken coverlet of which was drawn up and spread out, but could not entirely conceal the outline of a human figure, lying as flat as possible, evidently in the endeavour to escape observation.

'I will sit down awhile,' said the Marquis, in the cheerful voice of a person who has no unpleasant thought in his mind, 'and contemplate this master-work.'

As he said this he took up a pillow, its white covering trimmed with wide lace, and laid it on the spot where he thought the face of the concealed person must be, and placed himself upon it with all the weight of his somewhat bulky figure, whilst he placed his right hand upon the chest of the reclining form, and pressed on it with all his force.

Without heeding the involuntary, frightful, and convulsive heavings--the death-throes of his wretched victim--the Marquis exclaimed, in a calm, firm voice,--

'How beautifully that picture is finished! How noble and chaste does not the lovely penitent look, all sinner as she was, with her rich golden locks waving over that neck and those shoulders whiter than alabaster, while these graceful hands are clasped, and these contrite, tearful eyes seem gazing up yonder, whence alone mercy and pardon can be obtained! One could almost become a poet in gazing on so splendid a work of art. But ah! I never had the happy talent of an improvisatore. In place, therefore, of poetizing, I will tell you something that happened yesterday. Our little friend Giulio Balzetti took me round the Magdalene Church; and, whilst we were wandering about, he pointed out a particular spot to me, and bade me stand quite still there, telling me that *there* might be overheard what was said at another spot at some distance in the church. And he was right. At that other place stood the confessional No. 6. I had hardly placed myself on the marble flag indicated to me, than I heard a charming voice--God knows who it was speaking!--but she was confessing the sorrows of her heart and her little sins to the holy father. She had a husband, she said, whom she loved--yes, she loved him, and he loved her: he was very kind to her, and left her much at liberty; in short, she gave the husband credit for all sorts of good qualities, but, unfortunately, she had fallen in love with another man! She did not mention his name. I should like to have heard it. He must be one of our handsome young cavaliers about the town. And this other loved her, too--she could not help it, poor thing!--and so she found room for him in her heart as well as for the husband. This other one was so handsome, so pleasing, so fascinating!... Well ... if her husband did not know what was going on, he could not be vexed, and ... it would do him no harm. So she had promised to admit the lover early this morning. Do you hear? This is what the French dames call "passer ses caprices." At last, she begged the good priest to give her absolution beforehand. And he did so: he gave the absolution! What do you think of all this, my love?' said the Marquis, as he rose from the couch, where all was now still as death, 'Well,' he continued, in a jocular tone, 'our worthy priests are almost too complaisant and indulgent--at least, most of them. Our old Father Gregorio, however, would have taken *you* to task after a different fashion, if you ...'

He broke off abruptly, while he quietly laid the pillow in its own place, and deliberately turned down the embroidered coverlet. It was the architect Giulio Balzetti whom the Marquis beheld: he had ceased to breathe!

'Have you been to confession lately, my Laura?' asked the Marquis. There was no answer.

'Is it long since you have been to confession?' he asked, in a louder and sterner voice.

'No!' replied the young woman, in the lowest possible tone.

'Apropos,' said the Marquis, as he covered the frightfully distorted and blue face of the corpse with the coverlet, 'shall we not go to the grand festival at the church to-day? The procession begins exactly at twelve o'clock. I shall order the carriage--we really must not miss it.'

He returned to the dressing-room. The Marchioness was sitting in a large cushioned lounging-chair, the thick tresses of her dark hair hanging negligently down, her lips and cheeks as pale as death, and her hands resting listlessly on her lap.

'What is the matter, my dear child?' asked the Marquis, inwardly triumphing at her distress, but with fair and friendly words upon his lips. 'You have risen too early, my little Laura; and you have also fatigued yourself in trying to dress without assistance. Where is Pipetta? I shall ring for her now.' He pulled the bell-rope--approached his wife--slightly kissed her brow--and then left her apartments.

At mid-day, when all the bells of the churches were pealing, the Marquis's splendid state carriage, with four horses adorned with gilded trappings, stood before the gate of his palace, and a crowd of richly-dressed pages, footmen, and grooms, were in waiting there. Presently the Marquis appeared in his brilliant court costume, with glittering stars on his breast, his hat in one hand, whilst with the other he led his young and beautiful but deadly-pale wife. With the utmost attention he handed her down the marble steps, and while her countenance looked as cold and stony as that of a statue, his eyes flashed with a fire that was unusual to them. The servants hurried forwards, the carriage-door was opened, the noble pair entered it, and it drove off towards the town. In the crowded streets the foot passengers turned round to gaze at it, and exclaimed to each other, 'There go a happy couple!'

The architect had disappeared. No one suspected that on the day of the grand festival he lay dead--a blue and terrible-looking corpse--amidst boots and shoes, at the bottom of a noble young dame's wardrobe; or that, the following night, without shroud or coffin, his body was secretly transported by the lady's faithful servants to a neighbouring mountain, and there thrown into a deep cave. But the lady paid a large sum to the convent of the Magdalens for the sake of his soul's repose.

The monk Gregorio--the accommodating and favourite confessor of the fashionable world--was also soon after missing. But *he* was not dead--he lingered for some years in a subterranean prison belonging to a monastery of one of the strictest orders: a punishment to which he had been condemned through the influence of the Marquis d'Arena.

That the confessional No. 6 was removed, will be easily believed.

The Marquis never alluded to these events before his wife. When they appeared in public together, as also in society at his own home, he treated her with respect, often with attention. But he never again spoke to her in private, nor did he ever again enter those apartments which had once been the scene of so dreadful a tragedy.

THE ANCESTRESS; OR, FAMILY PRIDE FROM THE SWEDISH OF THE LATE BARONESS KNORRING

I

Adelgunda was one of the most beautiful creatures ever moulded by the great Master's hand, and one on whom He might deign to look with the same paternal complacency as Pygmalion looked on his Galathea.

Adelgunda was also as the apple of their eye to her father and mother; but not the less did they bring her up with the utmost strictness and severity, in the awful loftiness of their aristocratic principles, which made no allowance for a single error, a single imperfection, a single weakness even, among any who belonged to them. Everyone was to be super-excellent, and supremely high-bred like their ancestors; for their ancestors had only *virtues*, their failings being entombed with their bodies. The slightest infringement of the stately decorum, the formal propriety--and, to the honour of their ancestors we must add--the rectitude, the loyal and chivalric conduct of these worthies, called forth as unmerciful punishment as a heinous fault. And Adelgunda, from her earliest infancy, learned to form grand ideas about her noble, ancient, and opulent family; it was impressed on her mind that she would be very degenerate indeed if she did not resemble all those long departed, and now mouldering dames and damsels, whose portraits hung in long rows in the great picture-gallery, as a large old-fashioned apartment was called, which, in spite of accidental fires, of repairs and renovations in the old baronial castle, had preserved unaltered its antique appearance since the middle of the sixteenth century.

In her infancy, Adelgunda had often been taken into this venerable saloon, and, counting with her five small fingers, she could repeat the names of all those haughty-looking, long-bearded cavaliers, equipped in heavy armour, or these stiff, richly-dressed nobles, most of them decorated with jewelled orders, or other tokens of a high worldly position; and these grand-looking ladies, encased in whalebone and stiff corsets, with towering powdered heads and magnificent jewellery, evincing the wealth of the family. These ladies and gentlemen hung, as has been said, in straight rows on each side of the long, narrow, dark, oak-paneled hall; and they were all half-length portraits in oval or almost square frames, the gilding of which had long since faded into a sort of a brownish-yellow cinnamon tint. But at the end of the hall, between two deep Gothic windows, with small old-fashioned panes of glass, there hung alone in state the great *ancestress*, or founder of the family--a tall, dark, stern-looking woman, whose countenance was grave, austere, and almost menacing, though the features, when narrowly examined, were regular and beautiful.

In contrast to the half-length portraits around, this picture was almost colossal in size; and the noble lady it represented, who in Roman Catholic times had ended her days as the Abbess of a convent, stood there so stately and so stiff in the close black garb, with the unbecoming white linen band across her forehead, and with one hand, in which she held a crucifix, resting on a dark-looking stand, on which a missal, a skull, and a rosary, lay near each other, the other hand hung carelessly down by her side, and almost reached the lower portion of the picture-frame, which seemed considerably darker and more time-worn than all the rest. This picture was painted on thick wood, or on canvas stretched on wood, it was not certain which, but everyone knew that it was as heavy as lead--and so it proved to be.

The likeness of the patriarch of the family--of the father of the race--painted to correspond in size and everything else to that of the high-born lady above mentioned, had in former days hung also in this saloon, but had been destroyed in a fire which had taken place between the years 1740 and 1750, so that the stern imperious-looking dame now occupied the place of honour alone.

Her parents had never omitted, when they accompanied Adelgunda into the picture gallery, to take her up first to one, then to another of the noble ladies whose lineaments adorned the walls, saying, 'How fortunate for you if you could be as good as *this* ancestress of yours was--as clever as *that* one--as beautiful as *she* was--as dutiful and affectionate as *yon* lady!' Adelgunda would fix her eyes on each by turns, and every time she looked at them her desire to resemble them increased. But the great gloomy portrait of the tall dark lady always awakened a thrill of terror in the little girl's mind. This was partly owing to the tales with which the servants frightened her about this harsh, awful-looking abbess, partly to her being obliged, whenever she was naughty, to go into the sombre apartment where the picture was, and, curtseying before it, to beg pardon of the stern, threatening figure.

With her tearful looks fixed upon it, she had often fancied that the eyes of the portrait moved; but it was a still greater trial to poor Adelgunda, when she had been guilty of some great offence, to be condemned, as a punishment, to stand for a quarter of an hour, or half-an-hour, under the dreaded portrait with her back to it.

There was a tradition in the family that many, many years back, during the lifetime of one of the more ancient lords of the castle, a little girl, a member of the race, who was undergoing a similar punishment, distinctly felt the terrible lady's hand, which hung unemployed by her side, stretch over the picture-frame and seize roughly hold of her hair. The recollection of that tradition was martyrdom to Adelgunda when this most dreaded penance was inflicted on her; and on one occasion, when her conscience was not of the clearest, and she had cried herself almost into a fever from fright, she fancied that she actually felt a grasp at her little golden tresses.

It is easy to imagine how anxious, in consequence of all this, Adelgunda was to avoid committing any faults, and with what terror the picture inspired her. And even in riper years, when she began to lay aside her childish dress and childish ideas, and when reason told her that a painted figure could have no more power or influence than any other inanimate object, she still looked with a certain degree of awe upon the portrait of her frowning ancestress, especially when her conscience told her that she had been guilty of any slight indiscretion; while, on the contrary, she felt some pleasure at gazing on the other family pictures, which all seemed to smile upon her.

But years and time wore on, and the aristocratic bones of Adelgunda's proud, high-born parents were laid in the dust to mingle with the honoured remains of the old stock. She was then still in her minority, and found a new home with a kind aunt, who had resided too short a time under the same roof with the ancestral portraits, and in the place which had been the cradle of their race, to have imbibed their exaggerated family pride.

The estate, which was entailed, with everything belonging to it, including the much-prized portrait, passed in trust, for future generations, to Adelgunda's only brother, of whom we purposely have not spoken, that we might not be obliged to give an account of all the exaggerated ideas of the consequence of his family which his father and mother had diligently and zealously laboured to imprint on the mind of their son--the only male scion of that ancient house, which was now threatened with speedy extinction--he who, after them, was alone to represent the glory of their time-honoured ancestry. What precepts and exhortations he, the only son and last hope, received under his progenitor's portrait--what deference and devotion were inculcated to the name of the haughty-looking abbess, whose severe virtue and pious deeds were held to reflect honour on her descendants--what aristocratic ideas and exclusive principles were there engrafted on his soul, we will not stop to relate--they would be incomprehensible to many, and do not require to be dwelt on in our short tale.

In the aunt's cheerful, hospitable, pleasant, light modern villa quite another tone prevailed, and quite another mode of life from that within the solid walls of the old baronial castle or under its gloomy roof. At Adelgunda's age new impressions are soon received, new associations and new ideas are welcomed with avidity, and seldom fail to influence the mind. Adelgunda--truth obliges us to confess--soon forgot a very stringent and important paragraph in the paternal and maternal lectures--forgot the faithful portraits of the defunct females of her noble house, and even the threatening glance--the dark eye that shone from beneath the white linen fillet of the haughty abbess--forgot them all amidst new-born and overflowing happiness in the arms of an adored and adoring husband, a young naval officer, rich in all nature's brightest gifts, and standing high in the opinion of the world, but on whom the great ancestress would certainly never have permitted her hand to be bestowed, had she known of the matter; for his patent of nobility was not mouldy from age, was not even made out, and still worse, was not likely ever to be drawn up, because he did not feel the slightest wish ever to possess one.

Adelgunda, nevertheless, felt unspeakably happy, and her noble brother, to whom the family mode of thinking had descended as an heirloom in conjunction with the entailed property, winked at the plebeian match--partly because he well knew that Adelgunda's very limited portion would never tempt any among the needy and impoverished of his own class to lay their hearts at her feet--partly because it was the preservation of the family name and tree in his own person that lay nearest to his heart, not the offshoots from the female line--and partly that, though he was a proud man, and unflinching in his aristocratical notions, he had a kind heart, was fondly attached to his sister, rejoiced in her happiness, and was well aware how much superior in character his estimable brother-in-law was to the generality of the young men of the day.

But for himself, this brother and lord of the castle sought a spouse who should entwine no vulgar burgher twig around the fair branches of his genealogical tree, but one who counted as many generations as other good qualities; for ancient lineage is not apt, like wealth, to corrupt the heart, and Adelgunda's sister-in-law was truly an amiable lady.

Again the lordly halls of the ancient castle became the abode of domestic happiness; and it was admitted that it could not be otherwise, for not one alone, but many of the old servants who had passed into the service of the heir of entail, and who were not notorious for their superstition, had clearly and distinctly observed that the first time the young countess entered the picture gallery, the majestic ancestress had relaxed her stern lips almost into a smile of approbation, which had never happened but once before--in the year 1664, on a similar occasion; a remarkable event, which had been recorded by the chaplain of the castle, with many subscribing witnesses, in a document which was preserved like a holy relic amidst the family's most valued papers, parchments, and deeds.

When the young count and countess were happily wedded, and comfortably settled at the castle, which however, did not happen until about five years after Adelgunda's marriage to her delightful naval hero, the brother and sister felt a strong wish to meet once more under the paternal roof. And Adelgunda's husband promised that on his return in autumn from an expedition in which he was then engaged, he, his wife, and their little son, a boy about four years of age, should without any delay accept of the count's invitation, and make the visit so much desired by all parties--even by the young countess, Adelgunda's sister-in-law, who was by no means a stranger to her. They had been friends in childhood, indeed were distantly related to each other; for it so happens that almost all the families amongst the most ancient of the Swedish nobility are connected by ties of consanguinity.

At length the long-looked-for day arrived, and Adelgunda beheld, with tears of mingled joy and sorrow, the grey old towers of the castle where she was born, and where she had spent her earliest years--those years which, on comparing them with the subsequent epochs of our life, we denominate the gayest and the happiest. Adelgunda and her husband, who had had a long day's journey, arrived late in the evening at the castle, and were shortly after conducted to their sleeping-rooms, a suite of lofty arched apartments in one of the farthest towers, and in the olden time the principal guest-chambers, but which did not bear the best of reputations as regarded spectres, midnight noises, groans, rattling of chains, and the like horrors. Adelgunda had all her life entertained great respect for, but also no little fear of, these apartments; and those feelings were probably heightened by an old tradition which averred that some most extraordinary and mysterious events had taken place in these chambers. Some pretended to know that one of these apartments, which along with the picture-gallery had remained most unchanged during the lapse of years, had served as the bridal-chamber for the great ancestress of the family; at any rate, there was something that savoured of awe and discomfort about them.

Never in her life had Adelgunda slept in any of these gloomy apartments, and in former days nothing would have induced her to do so; but now, with her brave, bold sailor by her side, she smiled at her old childish fears,--at least when he laughed at her recital of them. She would not, however, on any account, allow her little Victor to sleep in the first antechamber with the trembling waiting-maid, but placed the child's crib close to her own bed, and often during the long, dark, and stormy autumnal night, when the wind shook the panes of glass, and howled through the adjacent forest, and she was awakened by its violence, she turned quickly, and with a beating heart, towards the child, leaned over his little bed, and felt unhappy until she had ascertained that her darling was sleeping soundly and peacefully.

'Well!' said her husband the next morning, when the sun was already pretty high in the heavens, and cast his cheerful rays through the narrow casements of these haunted chambers--'well, dearest Adelgunda, have you heard or seen any spectre last night--been visited in any way by a ghost?'

'No,' she replied laughingly, as the bright sunshine restored her courage; there was but one spirit near me last night--one dear, good spirit;' and she embraced her husband.

'And you, Annette?' cried the incredulous visitor to the poor waiting-maid, 'I hope you have not been disturbed by the ghosts either?'

But Annette, who was half-dead from fear, asserted that she had not closed her eyes the whole night; that she had distinctly heard sighs and groans, and heavy footsteps up and down the floor; and there had been many other frightful things that she could not describe.

Now, in the cheering daylight, Adelgunda laughed heartily at these *fancies*, as she called them; but the previous night she would not have done so,--at least not with a heart so much at ease.

'I wonder what his uncle and aunt will say of my little Victor, now that he is nicely dressed, and not so sleepy and cross as he was last night, after that long fatiguing journey!' said Adelgunda to Annette, with a mother's pride in her pretty boy, and while they were both engaged in arranging his curly hair, and putting on his handsome new green dress.

Adelgunda's husband had risen early and gone out to stroll round the old castle, and the former young lady of the mansion, who had now become a wife and mother, took up her little son in her arms to go down to her sister-in-law, who had already sent to inquire how she had slept, and to let her know that breakfast was ready.

Humming an air, Adelgunda proceeded with her light burden through the dear old well-remembered passages where her very footsteps echoed, until she came close to the door which opened into the picture-gallery; she then stopped, seized suddenly with a strong impulse to enter it, while a strange, sad foreboding of evil filled her heart. Influenced, as it were, by an invincible power over which she had no control, she laid her hand upon the lock, turned it, and stood, she scarcely knew how, in presence of the mute family, who seemed gazing on her from both sides. Adelgunda's heart beat quickly; recollections from her childhood and her youthful days began to rush back on her. These aristocratic feelings, which had so long slumbered, began to start up in her mind, and she dared not look towards the terrible lady at the extreme end, for fear of meeting her angry, implacable glance.

'That is a pretty lady! And there is another nice lady! What a grand gentleman! and see, yonder is a fine gentleman, too!'

Such were little Victor's exclamations, as Adelgunda went slowly with him past all these well-known portraits of uncles and aunts, grandmothers, great-grandmothers, and other members of the family, all long since asleep in their graves.

'But, oh, mother, look!' cried Victor, as he first caught sight of the largest; 'see how horrible that one up yonder looks! See, mother, how that tall woman there on the wall frowns down at us!' And Victor knit his little brows, and drew in his small mouth, to make his face look very terrible in return.

'Oh, do not speak so--do not speak so!' exclaimed his mother, trying in vain to hush the child. 'On the contrary,' she added, in a faltering voice, 'she is an excellent lady, and very kind to all good, well-behaved children. We will go up yonder, and beg her pardon and her blessing.'

'No, no!' screamed Victor, kicking his little legs with all his might; 'I won't have anything to do with her: she looks as cross as if she would bite me.'

'Again his mother entreated Victor to be a reasonable, good boy, and by that time they stood under the great lady's picture. A tremor crept over Adelgunda as she encountered that austere, repulsive look, and involuntarily she dropped her eyes beneath it. But reason soon triumphed; she approached closer to the portrait, and said to her little son, whom she still held in her arms, 'Now we shall say good morning to that lady;' and she curtseyed herself, and bent with her hand the obstinate little head; 'and we shall beg her to look kindly and gently down upon us, for your dear, good papa's sake, and we will kiss her hand.' And Adelgunda kissed the hand in the picture that was hanging down; but when she attempted to raise the child's face up towards the hand, the little fellow, in whose infantine breast was aroused a portion of his father's bold spirit, and perhaps impetuous temper, and who, though somewhat frightened, felt his courage rising, and was, withal, extremely angry, struggled furiously, clenched his little fist, and instead of kissing the great lady's drooping hand, thumped it with all his might--and at that moment he was strong enough.

II

Adelgunda's brother and sister-in-law waited in vain for her appearance at the breakfast-table. She came not! But at length the startling intelligence was brought to them that a strange, frightful noise had been heard in the picture-gallery. No one knew what was the cause of it, for no one had dared to venture in to see what had happened, but now every one rushed in. A cloud of dust, a heap of mortar and wood was before them; and a sight so dreadful, so shocking, so appalling, met their eyes, that every heart was like to break.

But only one heart *did* break, for notwithstanding his strength of mind--his unconquerable spirit--his undeniable fortitude, the bereaved husband and father almost sank beneath the frightful calamity that had suddenly deprived him of the wife he adored, and the child on whom all his hopes were centred. Yet he was the first--the only one who had sufficient energy, and presence of mind to drag the lifeless remains of his wife and son from under the destroying weight of the heavy portrait.

It was a frightful event, and made a great sensation. A rotten rope, and the mouldering state of the wall which should have upheld the enormously heavy wooden frame, had done all the evil.

The naval officer passed over distant seas to many a foreign land--the world was all before him, but he never forgot what he had lost.

The picture of the awful ancestress met with little injury in its fall; but several years elapsed before it was hung up again in its former place. It was, however, at length restored to its old position, but fastened with new rope, and everything necessary to make it more secure. The dreadful occurrence was beginning to be forgotten, and the brotherly affection which had somewhat cooled, seemed to have displayed itself sufficiently in having banished the lofty dame for some years to a lumber-room. She could not always be left there! So at length she hung in her old place again, as stern, as frowning as formerly. And the count, who had now become an old man, generally when he alluded to the terrible event, reasonably ascribed it to natural causes. But, once upon a time, when he observed his youngest daughter, a girl not much more than sixteen years of age, casting *furtive* and *rather friendly* glances at a young man, the son of a country parson, who, on account of his handsome person and pleasant manners, was often received at the baronial castle,--when he saw this, by means of some sidelong looks with the corner of his eye, which were not perceived by the young couple, then he took his daughter by the hand, led her silently and solemnly into the picture-gallery, walked with her up to the replaced portrait of their great ancestress, and said with the gravity of an anxious father, and the dignity of an aristocratic nobleman,--

'Beware, my daughter! Remember the fate of your aunt!'

These words were all he uttered.

'And this happened in the nineteenth century, and here in our fatherland? 'Such an inquiry will assuredly be made by one or other of our readers. But we will not answer it ourselves; we shall only advise the inquirer to address himself to the descendants of *one of the most ancient families in Scania,* and ask *them* whether it be true or not.

THE MAN FROM PARADISE[10]
A Comic Tale FROM THE DANISH OF HANS CHRISTIAN ANDERSEN

There was a widow, once upon a time--
Yet stop--with *truth* we must commence our rhyme--
She *had* been such, but now another spouse
Had sought her love, and won the widow's vows.

One evening she was quite alone at home
(For the best husbands sometimes like to roam);
She sat, her cheek reposing on her hand,
The tea-things spread upon the table, and
The kettle singing by, or on the fire--
A sort of a monotonous steam lyre:
Her thoughts from this low world of fogs had flown
Up to the husband she first called her own;
She could not *quite* the dear, kind soul forget--
And ah! the other one was absent yet.
'But thou art happy now,' she cried--'in case
In Abraham's bosom thou hast found a place:
Thou pitiest us, in these rooms close and old,
Where one so often gets a cough or cold.'

Then into a brown study she did fall,
When suddenly some sounds her thoughts recall;
She hears a gentle knocking at the door;
She starts--looks at the roof, then at the floor--
Then peers into each corner, as she cries,
'Well--who is there?' To be right brave she tries,

But truth to tell, she almost shook with fear
To see some ghost, or corpse-like form appear.
Another knock--then in the doorway stood
No spectre, but a youth of flesh and blood
'Twas an apprentice who had run away
From work, and chose from town to town to stray:
The rogue lived by his wits as best he might,
For nought he scrupled at--except to fight.

The quondam widow very soon perceived
The intruder was not what she had believed--
That he was mortal, not a form of air.
She questioned whence he came, and also where
He might be bound. 'I'm on my way,' said he,
'To Paris, madam, *viâ* Germany.'
With joyous heart she listened to his tale,
And then she placed before him meat and ale,
Kindly inviting him to eat and drink;
While she exclaimed, 'How very strange to think
That you to Paradise are journeying on!--
Why, that's the land where my first husband's gone!
Please give my love to him, our daughter's, too,
And--*his successor's compliments,* will you?'

Quickly the knave observed that the good dame
In her geography was rather lame--
That *Paradise* with *Paris* she confounded.
And though one moment he looked up astounded,
The next into her droll conceit he fell,
Saying, 'Oh, yes! I know the good man well.'
'What! have you really been already there?'
She cried. 'Then say, how does the dear one fare?'
'Ah! very badly. 'Tis a tale of woe!
I was up there about a month ago.
A sort of a dog's life the poor thing led,
Early he had to rise--get late to bed;
Worked hard, and scarce a stitch of clothing had.

His shroud and grave-clothes from the first were bad;
They very soon wore out, and now he goes
Without a coat, and with bare legs and toes.'
These words went like a dagger to her heart;
She shuddered--groaned--then, with a sudden start,
She rose, and soon an ample bundle made
Of linen, coats, warm woollen socks; and said,
Whilst with big tear-drops both her eyes looked dim.
'This package, sir, I pray you take to him.
Tell the poor fellow I shall send him more
By the first opportunity--a store
I'll surely send. Oh dear! oh dear! 'tis sad
His fate in yonder place should be so bad!'

The rogue had stuffed quite to his heart's content,
So, taking up the bundle, off he went;
But first he thanked her for the food, and vowed
The clothes she sent should soon replace the shroud.
Long, long she sits, her eyes still full of tears;
The absent husband now at length appears
('Tis to the *second* one that I allude--
The *first*, as has been shown, was gone for good).

'Well, I have curious tidings for your ear--
A man from Paradise has just been here;
He knew poor *Thi--is* there.' (Such was the name
Of him who was first husband to the dame.)
And thereupon, with a most serious face,
She told him all that had just taken place.
The husband, when he heard her, smelled a rat,
But only saying he would have a chat
Himself with the great traveller, he sent
For his best horse, and after him he went.

'Twas a sweet night, the moon was shining clearly--
Just such a night as poets love most dearly;
The nightingales were pouring forth their notes,

The owls were exercising, too, their throats;
But, what was better still, he found the track
The thief had ta'en, and hoped to bring him back.
Thieves, by the way, like the moon's silver rays
Far better than the sun's meridian blaze.
And now, how fared it with the thief himself,
Thus making off with his ill-gotten pelf?

He spied a man, who like old Nick was riding,
And felt that he was in for a good hiding;
Therefore into a neighbouring ditch he flung
The burden that across his back had slung,
Then casting himself down upon a bank,
Quite in a lounging attitude he sank,
And gazing on the clear calm skies above,
He sang some ditty about ladies' love.
Up comes the rider at a rapid trot--
The pace had made him and his steed both hot--
And asked abruptly, reining in his grey,
If he had seen a rascal pass that way,
Who on his shoulders a large bundle bore--
A horrid thief he was, the horseman swore.
'Why, yes,' was the reply. 'I have just seen
A fellow with long legs pass by--I ween
It is the same you seek; for he looked round
Soon as your horse's footfall on the ground
Was heard--and then, as quickly as he could,
He fled to hide himself in yonder wood.
If you make haste, you there will catch him soon.'
The horseman thanked him much and craved a boon--
It was to hold his steed, while in pursuit
He went himself into the wood on foot.
'Twas granted, and the husband rushed among
The bushes tall--while the thief laughing sprung
Upon the horse; he took the bundle too,
And fast away he rode, or rather flew.

Angry, fatigued, and scratched till he was sore,
The husband came, his bootless errand o'er.
Fancy what was his grief, his rage, to find
The horse he thought he left so safe behind,
Gone too! he cried, 'Hey! hey!' its name he called,
But all in vain he shouted and he bawled--
The clever thief the faster rode away.
There was no creature near on whom to lay
The blame; so the poor foolish dupe abused
The moon, for having thus her light misused.
Home on his weary legs he had to trudge;
His steed to the vile thief did he not grudge!

'Well, did you find him?' asked his smiling wife.
He answered, in a tone subdued, 'My life,
I did. I found him, and--and--for *your* sake,
Our best, our swiftest horse I let him take,
That he with greater speed might find his way.'
The dame smiled on him, and in accents gay
Exclaimed, 'O best of husbands! who could find
Your equal--one so thoughtful, wise, and kind!'

MORAL

The moral of this story shows,
Though knaves on women oft impose,
That men are sometimes quite as *green*,
But hold their tongues themselves to screen.

FOOTNOTES:

Footnote 1: A Danish title, signifying councillor of justice.

Footnote 2: Danish mile, equal to about 4 3/4 English miles.

Footnote 3: Fourteen and a quarter English miles.

Footnote 4: 'To give a basket,' in Danish, signifies a refusal.

Footnote 5: A Danish title.

Footnote 6: 'Aprilsnarrene.' A Danish vaudeville.

Footnote 7: The ceremony of Confirmation is deemed of the highest importance in Denmark, and is never neglected in any rank of life, from the prince to the peasant.

Footnote 8: For these, and 'Octavianus,' see Ludwig Tieck's works. They have been translated into Danish by Adam Oehlenschlæger.

Footnote 9: A town of Sicily, in the Val di Mazzara, on the site of the ancient Agrigenum, the magnificent ruins of which are still to be seen.

Footnote 10: Manden Fra Paradiis. En komisk Fortælling.